ALSO BY ILIANA XANDER

Love, Mom

ALL EYES ON HIM

ILIANA XANDER

Poisoned Pen
PRESS

Published by Poisoned Pen Press, an imprint of Sourcebooks
1935 Brookdale RD, Naperville, IL 60563-2773
(630) 961-3900
sourcebooks.com

Originally self-published in 2025 by Iliana Xander.

Cataloging-in-Publication data is on file with the Library of Congress.

Printed and bound in the United States of America.
LSC 10 9 8 7 6 5 4 3 2 1

PROLOGUE

I loved you. Up until the day you decided to kill our baby.

Our unborn baby—but still.

My hands shake, and I try to hold back tears as I toss several pieces of clothing into a canvas bag sitting on our bed.

I need to get out of here, fast.

"Take the Mercedes," you said on the phone as I walked out of the clinic earlier. "It drives like a dream. You'll be at your parents' in no time."

At my parents', right. Now that you think I went through with the abortion, you don't care what I do or where I go.

When I told you a week ago that I was pregnant, your only words were, "We can't. We are not ready. My business takes all my time. I can't be distracted."

I can. I *am* ready. But it's too late for you to fix what your words have broken, what you've done to me in the last week.

You are a brilliant man. You'll go far. You always get what you want at *any* cost, and I've found out some things about your business that make me uneasy. I've always sensed a darkness in you. It trickled into our life little by little until I realized you weren't the man I fell in love with a year ago.

And now we are here...

You were the one who booked an appointment at the private clinic for abortions. You paid for it. You drove me there this morning, sat with me while we waited for the doctor. With no mention of the week I'd spent telling you that I didn't want to do it. That I'd be fine. That I'd take care of the baby. If only you had let me.

Instead, for the last week, you'd kept me prisoner. You'd sedated me with some medication for days, making me compliant.

"It's for the best," you whispered before the nurse led me away.

And you left. "I have to go. I have a meeting. Take a cab home when you're done."

You hoped I'd be a coward, still high on whatever sedative you'd pumped into me. But I didn't go through with it. When the nurse sat me down, the tears started spilling down my face. I told her that I didn't want to do it. That it wasn't my choice.

When I walked out of that room two hours later, I was calm, proud of what I *didn't* do.

I just need to get some personal belongings from your place, drive away, and never see you again, never tell you that our child will grow up without knowing its father. I shouldn't be driving after you've been drugging me for days, but I need to get away from you.

My shaky hands almost drop my laptop as I shove it into a computer bag. I pick it up, together with the canvas bag, and hurry out of the house.

My phone rings.

It's you.

My stomach drops, dread coiling inside me. In one week, you turned from a loving partner into a cruel monster, and my heart thuds in panic when I pick up the phone.

"Everything all right?" you ask, traffic noise in the background. Your business is more important than me or the baby we could've had together.

"Fine. I'm fine."

There's a weight in my chest, a tension, a feeling that you know. That you *suspect* something. I don't remember the moment I began to be afraid of you.

"I will see you soon," you say. "I'll pick you up from your parents' in a couple of days."

No, you won't. "Yes, of course."

My parents' house in upstate New York is only a three-hour drive from your place in Vermont. I never want to see this place again, but now I fear that I won't be far enough away from you.

"Once you are on the highway," you say, "it's a breezy ride. No cars. You'll fly. I love you, Emily."

Emily… You don't call me that. You call me Em. Emily is for when you are upset or withdrawn.

"I love you too," I say, though this time, I'm lying.

The drive through the Adirondack Mountains is easy. I have time to think about what to do next, how to live on. Without you. A single mother.

It's a calming drive. Getting away from you feels like freedom. An hour into the drive, my car is winding down the mountain highway, but when I brake, trying to slow down, the brake pedal gives with little resistance.

My stomach sinks—I'm going downhill, struggling to keep control of the car that's gaining speed.

A turn is looming ahead. A cliff…

I press the brakes again, but the pedal sinks to the floor. Easily. Far too easily… My heart pounding, I jam it as hard as I can, but I already know it won't work.

Your words flash in my mind. *"You'll fly."*

Dread washes over me like a tide.

The car speeds up, gaining momentum, careening toward the sharp turn ahead.

And then I fly…

1

NATALIE

"Brain dead?" I whisper and feel the omelet I had for breakfast forcing its way back out.

My friend Cara, lying motionless on a hospital bed, makes my stomach turn. A flashback of Lindsey's funeral hits me, stirring fresh pain.

The three of us moved to New York City nine years ago. Small-town girls. Big dreams.

Then there was just Cara and me.

Now, another one of my best friends is fighting for her life.

"That's not what I said, Miss Olsen," says the detective who stands just a bit behind me, explaining what happened so routinely, like she does it every day for a living. "She's in a coma with little brain activity."

The detective is around my age. But her voice is low and abrasive, like she's recovering from a bad sore throat, which doesn't go with her pretty feminine looks.

"The doctor will be here shortly to explain everything,"

she continues. "They said your friend is likely to have some degree of amnesia if she recovers. It's the effect of the drug found in her system."

"What drug does *that*?" I choke out as I step closer to the hospital bed, afraid that, if I touch Cara, she will feel cold like a corpse.

"Think date-rape drug but five times stronger, with potentially lethal effects."

"Why?" I ask in a whisper.

"To find out why, we need to find the person who did that to her. We need your help."

"I already told you. I have no idea who he is."

"Assuming it's a *he*."

"Who else would it be? Like I said, we were at the club. We were drinking. She was talking to the red-haired guy I told you about. She never said his name, only that he was in the VIP section."

"Did you get a good look at him? Who was he with?"

"Don't know. She just said he was a VIP."

As well as, *"He is my jackpot. Soon, we'll get out of that hell-hole in Jersey. I promise, babe!"*

But the detective doesn't need to know that.

I'm still hungover from yesterday, and Cara… Well, Cara went home with a stranger and was found unconscious at a bus stop early this morning.

"So, let me get it straight," the detective says calmly. "She's been drinking. She's just met this guy. She doesn't know him. You don't even know his name. And you let your friend go home with him without a second thought?"

"Listen…" I close my eyes, trying to get my thoughts in order.

How do I explain without getting judged that Cara liked

to party, liked sex, liked money? She enjoyed hooking up with men.

Of course, the detective won't understand it. Her next words prove it.

"That's how young ladies end up unconscious at public bus stops at dawn. I'll tell you one thing, that was probably a lucky scenario for her, considering…"

I look at her over my shoulder, running into her indifferent gaze. "Considering what?"

"Considering she wasn't raped, as per the rape kit. No sexual intercourse in the last twenty-four hours. So why was she spiked with such a heavy drug? I have a feeling there's more to this story, Miss Olsen."

"Can't you check the club's cameras?"

"There's no crime, per se. There's no evidence pointing to the man from the club."

"So you are *not* investigating this?"

"We are interested for a different reason."

"What other reason can there be?" I snap, though there's no point arguing. I get it. *No crime, per se.*

"There's another young woman in this very hospital in a similar condition," the detective says. "Which was the result of the exact same drug. Except she has no brain activity."

My insides turn. "You think there's a connection?"

"Recently, there were two similar cases of women poisoned by the same drug. No leads. No evidence of what happened. The substance we are talking about is not a prescription drug. It's illegal in the States."

"Those other women didn't say what happened?"

"They never recovered."

Bile rises to my throat, but I push down the dread. It takes me a moment before I speak again. "What's the verdict on Cara's current state?"

"The doctors can't say yet. It hasn't been long enough. She needs to come to, talk, and go through a number of tests. It's fifty-fifty."

"What does that mean?"

"She recovers without a clear memory of the last several days. Or…"

It's the *or* that makes my stomach turn again.

Cara looks peaceful on the hospital bed, her heart monitor quietly beeping. Just like Lindsey before she passed. This is a screwed-up déjà vu that grips my emotions in an iron-like hold.

But hope is a trickster, often making us believe that we can beat the odds. Cara will. She will. *You've got it, babe.*

"Or she will have permanent brain damage," the detective says.

I bite down on my lower lip to stop the tears welling up in my eyes.

"We need to find the person responsible," I say, despite *no crime, per se.*

"Are you telling me *everything*, Miss Olsen?" the detective insists, making me feel as if *I'm* the criminal here.

She waits for the answer, but I'm done with this conversation.

"Well, think it over. Call me if you think of anything."

I ignore her and grit my teeth as she passes me her card and leaves without saying goodbye.

Detective Lesley Dupin, Jersey City Police Department, her card reads.

Whatever.

It's suddenly hard to breathe. Only now do I realize that my best friend might never recover. We might never have night-long chats again. No clubs. No dress-ups. No dreams of traveling the world. Or going to Greece. Or doing a road trip and camping out in the Appalachians.

First Lindsey. Now Cara. What have we done to deserve this?

I wipe away tears and pray for Cara to wake up. I have no clue who the man is that did this to her. He's a needle in the middle of the haystack that's New York City. So, how do I find a red-haired stranger who possibly injected my friend with a dangerous drug and dumped her at a bus stop?

2

NATALIE

On any given day, in a matter of seconds, Manhattan can become a death trap.

Both sides of Thirty-Fourth Street are packed with New Yorkers, already inching onto the pedestrian crossing, into the steady bumper-to-bumper traffic, despite the pedestrian signal still being red.

That's Manhattan. People and cars navigate the streets with jarring impatience.

My crappy mood doesn't match the sunny weather. The interview for the bartending position at the Hyatt went well. But despite my stellar résumé, my frequent job changes are a red flag.

The traffic light turns yellow, and someone is already pushing against me from behind, nudging me into the back of a young man in front of me. He's holding a coffee, his attention on the phone in his hand. His cologne is seductively bitter. Neatly combed light-brown hair, crisp white shirt, dress pants, and pointy leather shoes—he's probably a banker or something of the sort. He looks pristine even in the early September heat. Judging by how little attention he pays to the traffic, he is a native New Yorker.

He starts walking, drawing my attention to the green pedestrian light.

By instinct, I step forward.

Just then, the sound of screeching tires makes my head snap in the direction of a red Oldsmobile, which is making a sharp turn on a red light at full speed into our street.

Like ants, the pedestrians split in half, jumping back or jolting forward.

Except for the young man.

Without thinking, I grab him by the arm and yank him back out of the way of the car that misses him by an inch.

His coffee goes flying into the air. The car swipes the curb but, without stopping, speeds away.

"Jeez," he blurts out, turning to me with wide eyes.

The crowd surges forward, shouldering us, unfazed by the accident that was just prevented. But the strikingly blue eyes of the stranger hold me hostage.

He is charmingly handsome.

"Phew," Mr. Handsome exhales, his eyes roaming my face. "I think you just saved my life." He chuckles, his lips spreading in a gorgeous smile.

"Or spared you a hospital bill," I say.

Someone shoulders me, and I start walking, the man following alongside.

"At the very least!" he says excitedly, as if we have just witnessed a miracle. "Freaking drivers here. Insane, huh? I guess I need a new coffee," he says as he checks his empty to-go cup, walking with me shoulder to shoulder. "I owe you one."

"You don't owe me anything," I murmur.

But a coffee sounds good. I don't have a job. I can't splurge, or I won't have money for rent.

"Nick." Without stopping, the handsome stranger offers his hand for a shake.

"Natalie," I say as I shake it.

He nods toward a Starbucks. "Come on. Please, let me buy you a coffee."

He quickly checks his watch, and I have a feeling that this is not an invitation for a date, just a courtesy. But why not?

"There is better coffee than that," I say. He might not be a native New Yorker after all. I nod toward the PapaBean street stall. "Best coffee around. Ethiopian. Light roast."

He grins at me. "Oh, yeah?" His blue eyes seem even more vibrant as they catch the sunlight. "Whatever you say, boss. Come on." He beelines through the crowded street toward the kiosk. "I'll have whatever she does," he tells the middle-aged man with a mustache and an apron, and I place the order. "So, Natalie, what are you doing on this fine day? Besides saving lives and trashing my coffee taste?" he says in a smooth voice that could melt chocolate.

That grin of his is contagious, and I smile back. "Actually, I just left a job interview. I'm better at saving lives than keeping a job."

Nick laughs, the sound of it making my smile grow, even though by any definition, this is a crappy day for me. Not to mention my best friend has been in a coma for three days now.

"What kind of job are you looking for?" Nick asks.

I shrug. "At this point? Anything. Degree, no degree. Qualifications, no qualifications."

I gave up pursuing jobs for my business degree several

years ago. Turns out, bartending at upscale places pays better. That is, if you can keep the job.

"That bad, huh?"

"Yeah."

It's my own fault that I lost my previous gig at a tapas place for being too abrasive and rude—get that—to the rude Wall Street assholes who made sexist comments. On top of that, Cara hasn't shown any improvement. She is lucky, the doctor said, though she still hasn't come to.

Looks like I have to pay rent all on my own this month.

At the thought, my smile falters. I absently study the magazine stand on the side of the coffee kiosk, trying to stay away from negative thoughts.

That's when I see *him*.

There are plenty of red-haired men in New York. Forgettable, sure. Just not this face, with the peculiar tick of his right eyebrow, his green eyes staring at me from the cover of the magazine.

I swallow hard, frozen to the spot—it *is* him.

"Your coffee, young lady," Nick says next to me.

But my eyes are glued to the magazine, and I slowly pick it up from the stand.

There's no mistake—the face on the cover of the *Tech Weekly* magazine belongs to the guy Cara went home with after the club. He has a name—Geoffrey Rosenberg.

MAN OF THE YEAR.

THE CEO OF IXRESEARCH.

THE CRYPTO KING.

**AND THE NEWEST ADDITION TO
THE FORBES 40 UNDER 40.**

Cara's words ring in my ears. *"He's my jackpot."*
And possibly a predator, I add silently.

3

NATALIE

"Wow, so smitten you don't even want your coffee?"

The voice pulls me out of my stupor. Mr. Handsome is smiling at me, his eyes shifting from the magazine cover to me as I take the coffee from him.

He tips his chin at the cover. "You into cryptocurrency?"

"No, no," I respond.

I want to say that the man on the cover might have something to do with poisoning my best friend and possibly other women, but I hold my tongue. My heart starts pounding as my hand slides into my purse to search for my phone—I need to call the detective.

"My boss," Nick says.

"Huh?" I freeze, staring at him with a momentary shock.

His eyes motion toward the magazine cover. "That's my boss," he repeats with pride.

I knew he had something to do with the über-rich. "No way," I blurt out.

"Yeah. I'm his personal driver."

Oh. So, not a banker, after all.

"Must be nice," I say, shoving the magazine back onto the stand, intending to research the Man of the Year online as soon as I get home.

"Nice what?" Nick's brows draw together.

Driver or not, Nick must be making big bucks, judging by his crisp outfit and polished shoes.

"Working for a millionaire," I say. "Pays well?"

Nick chuckles. "I guess. He's a good guy. Filthy rich too."

The last words turn my thoughts by 180 degrees.

There's one thing that history has proven—the rich often get away with their crimes. Mr. Crypto-King-Rosenberg probably has enough funds to bribe the police and the entire justice system. Me calling the detective won't change a thing. Absolutely nothing will come out of it. Except— the thought sends shivers down my spine—I might end up just like Cara.

Right away, doubt creeps into my head. Why would a guy who is rich and famous, who is on the cover of a magazine, take a girl home and pump her with drugs, then let her go? According to the doctors, Cara had no signs of physical or sexual assault, not even a scratch. And that makes me wonder if this man on the cover has anything to do with it at all.

"Is the good guy hiring?" I joke without thinking, not sure why I even said that.

"No." Nick chuckles, but his expression instantly changes, as if a lightbulb has gone off in his head. "You know what? What job were you interviewing for?"

A bartender, I almost say, though I have a degree in business, but that doesn't pay the bills too well these days.

"Why?" I ask instead, so as not to give away too much.

"My boss is having a business party this weekend. With catering services and all that stuff. But one of his housekeepers is on emergency leave."

Nick scrunches up his face in what looks like pity.

Oh, wow. So he thinks I'm looking for *that* type of job.

I'm about to say something bitter to Nick, the hotshot driver. Sure, my simple white button-up, jeans, and my hair pulled back in a ponytail don't give the impression of me interviewing for a CEO's assistant. But a cleaning lady? Really?

I don't say that. Nick's gaze is not arrogant, not even a bit. It's sweet and expectant, and I realize he's actually trying to help.

"Are you asking me if I want to interview for a cleaning job at your boss's office?" I probe, wondering if he is joking after all.

"Not his office—his residence. It's in Jersey, twenty minutes or so outside the city."

Nick scrunches up his nose again. I get it—that's across the river in a different state. Coincidentally, I live in Jersey City, just across the river.

Nick shrugs. "It's a staff of six people plus me. A temporary position anyway. Just trying to help if you are interested."

I desperately need money. Like yesterday. "Won't it take forever for a background check?" I ask carefully. "An interview? A résumé?"

I really don't have time for that.

"Not if you know the right people," he says with a wink. "The least I can do for someone who saved my life. Would be nice to have a pretty face around."

I don't know what to say. This morning, when I left my apartment to take the train to Manhattan for an interview, a cleaning lady position wasn't even remotely an option. But this is not just any position. It might be fast money. And that's not even the draw. It's working for Geoffrey Rosenberg, the man who may or may not be involved in Cara's poisoning. If there's a chance to find out, it's right now.

I chew on the inside of my cheek in contemplation. "You are saying I can get a job before the weekend and get paid right after?"

Nick checks his watch. At that very moment, his phone rings, and he switches the coffee into his other hand to pick it up.

"I'm here," he answers, his face immediately acquiring a stern expression. "Yes, I'll be there in five. Had a little delay... Yes. No problem, boss."

His boss! He must be talking to the Man of the Year! It does something to my insides, which twist in unease.

"What time is the conference call?" He motions with two fingers for my phone as he keeps talking to his boss on the other end. I pass him my phone, and he types in a phone number and sends a text, Natalie, to himself.

"Call me later today," he mouths to me as he answers into the phone. "Understood... Yes... Yes. No problem."

He winks at me and starts walking away, disappearing into the sea of people.

If this isn't luck, I don't know what is. I have a chance to meet the Man of the Year in person, maybe get to know him, maybe find out what happened the night Cara was drugged.

Cleaning trash will be temporary. And if Rosenberg turns out to be trash? I'll figure out how to deal with him.

I just have to be very careful.

4

NATALIE

Despite having to save every penny for rent, I do end up buying the magazine with the red-haired devil on its cover. I need the picture of the Man of the Year to remind me that I can, in fact, track that predator if he turns out to be one.

Jersey City Heights is across the river from Manhattan. That's a fifteen-minute train ride. Cara and I have a car that we drove to the city from back home, but we only use it for out-of-town trips.

On the short train ride, I scan the article about Geoffrey Rosenberg. There's nothing much about his past, except that he dabbled in crypto and digital ventures after he dropped out of college. He reemerged on the cryptocurrency scene about a year ago. Since then, his company, IxResearch, has become the most successful cryptocurrency exchange in the US.

I don't know much about digital currency. And I definitely don't know how one starts a company that a year later is backed by investors from around the globe and valued at ten figures. Apparently, at the age of thirty-four, Geoffrey

Rosenberg is an entrepreneurial mastermind. He lives in Jersey. He rarely makes public appearances. He's charming, private, extremely intelligent. And his company is soon to go public, which, analysts project, will multiply its value by ten. That's tens of billions of dollars.

Apparently, just like many young millionaires, Mr. Rosenberg doesn't shy away from clubs or spiking young women.

Why?

The incident with Cara still doesn't make sense, but I'm itching to find out more about the man I suspect is responsible.

As soon as I arrive to my apartment, I move the Styrofoam wig head on the coffee table to the side and open my laptop, then clear the clothes off the couch to make room for myself to sit.

Our place is a tiny two-bedroom on the ground floor of a three-story brick row house. If it were me, this place would be pristine. But Cara is a costume designer. Every space in our apartment is occupied with fabric swatches, garments, and sequin strips. A pincushion model and a tailor's dummy stand in one corner, a mannequin in another. Cara is talented, but I wish she didn't have so many side hustles that make our apartment look like a dressing room for a burlesque show.

A scratching noise draws my attention to the cage sitting in the corner.

"Ugh, Trixy." I rise with a sigh and walk to the kitchen to grab a piece of lettuce and zucchini. We get the battered veggies for free from a small grocery store around the corner, just for Trixy.

Trixy is our pet rat. Smart, feisty, and honestly, quite useless, but I love her to death. She's entertaining to watch. The cage door lock broke some time ago, so now we have a treasure box holding it closed.

I feed Trixy, then hurry back to the computer.

"Geoffrey Rosenberg," I whisper as I search the internet.

There are dozens of articles about him, most only in connection with his venture, as well as several pictures of him from conferences and interviews with bloggers. All his social media accounts post strictly business info.

I spend two hours reading anything I find about the mysterious millionaire. I make myself instant noodles and absent-mindedly eat them as I scroll the internet.

There's very little info about Rosenberg's school and college years. He was raised by a single mom in Vermont. She passed away when he was a freshman in college. He dropped out, started exploring the digital currency world, and recently took the financial world by storm.

Someone on an online crypto forum thread posted a picture of him from his college years.

"Well, hello," I murmur as I study the twenty-year-old Geoffrey Rosenberg. He's come a long way from the skinny, unremarkable redhead he used to be.

But Rosenberg's past is not of much interest to me. His present is.

Trixy starts loudly rattling the cage. She does that often. She has a temper.

Cara jokes, "She's just like us back home. Trying to break out of the cage. Maybe, one day we'll set her free."

I close my eyes and hold my breath, feeling the tears coming on.

Cara, Lindsey, and me. We were so young when we moved to New York City. We tried so hard to make it big, to forget the gloomy little life we had in a small town in the crack of nowhere.

Cara has always been a troublemaker. Lindsey was the smartest of us three. A straight-A student in school. A full-ride college scholarship, unlike the low-income financial aid that Cara and I got. Unfortunately, terminal cancer has no regard for merits or lifetime goals.

Lindsey never made it to her twenty-third birthday.

I'd never been to a funeral until the day we buried Lindsey, back in our hometown, where the few people present glared at Cara and me as if we had stolen her away. Before leaving the cemetery, Lindsey's father paused in front of Cara and me and said angrily, "That city killed her."

Tears burn my eyes. Trixy goes still in her cage, as if feeling my sadness.

I can't lose Cara too. I don't want to be *the only one*. The only one to be alive. The only one to "take the world by storm," as we pledged nine years ago, driving the beat-up Toyota across the States on our way to the Big Apple. God, we were so naive.

I might be naive right now, but I need to figure out why Rosenberg did what he did to Cara. I need closure. I want revenge for Cara. That means I have to get to Rosenberg.

I pick up my phone and dial the handsome stranger, Nick. My call goes straight to his voicemail, so I send a text instead.

Me: Any update on the potential job for me? Thank you again for doing this. Hope to hear from you soon.

Nick responds in two minutes.

Nick: I'll let you know soon.

My optimistic mood deflates. "Soon" can't come soon enough, so I start cleaning the living room, moving Cara's current projects to her bedroom that barely has space. Even Lady Bunny and one of Alexander McQueen's models' poster on her bedroom wall have tchotchkes hanging around them.

When my phone dings with a text message notification, I dart toward it like a ninja.

> Nick: Tomorrow. 9 a.m. You will meet with Julien, the house manager.

An address follows, near Alpine, a wealthy area in Jersey—no surprise.

> Nick: The security guard at the gate will know who you are.

Security? I guess that makes sense, considering Rosenberg's wealth.

> Nick: See you tomorrow.

I dial his number, but he cuts the call.

> Nick: Can't talk, doll;)
> Me: Thanks, handsome! I really appreciate this! Anything else I need to know before I start?
> Nick: That place is a little uptight, but you'll be fine.

I've worked at plenty of uptight places that cater to the rich. It's the subtle undertone of the next message that makes me uneasy.

> Nick: Make sure you follow the rules.

DAY 1

5

NATALIE

The Splendors Mansion, says an elegant sign on the giant gate that conceals Geoffrey Rosenberg's house.

I stop my car in front of it. I didn't get a code to get in, so I pick up the phone, intending to text Nick, when the door of the security booth on the side of the gate opens and a large guard steps out.

I roll down the window. "I'm here for the job interview."

Close-shaven beard, square jaw that could crack walnuts, thick eyebrows just below a baseball hat—the security guy looks like a bulldog.

He stares at me with unmistakable disapproval, like I'm here to replace him.

"I don't think so," he says slowly. "Wait here."

He squeezes his six-foot bulky frame back into the security booth, checks something in a notepad, then steps out and shakes his head. "There's nothing about you or any interview in my memo." He swings his forefinger in the air. "Turn around."

"This is a misunderstanding," I say, then dial Nick.

He picks up right away. "Hey, doll."

"Nick, I'm here, at the mansion, but the security guy says he doesn't know anything about the interview."

"Ugh, give me a sec. Stay there."

He hangs up, and I apologize to the hostile security guy. "Give me a moment, please. I'm Natalie, by the way. What's your name?"

He stalls, his iguana gaze on me like I just personally insulted him. "Dave."

I tense and stare at my hands on the steering wheel, waiting.

His phone rings. "Understood," he answers curtly. "Yes. Yes. No problem, sir." He hangs up and shifts his glare to me. "Park on the west side of the building. Use the staff entrance. You are going to talk to Julien," he says with reluctance as if I'm in the wrong here. He squeezes himself back into the booth and opens the gate.

"Thank you, Dave!" I call, hoping that this is the only hiccup at the job that hasn't even started yet.

I drive in slowly through the opening gate, checking the rearview mirror, and see Dave on the phone again, his head turned toward me as he watches me drive.

"Whatever, man," I murmur. "I'm here for a job, just like you."

But my mood lightens when I drive up to the mansion.

Well, well.

The Splendors is a two-story modern mansion with a fountain at the front and a vast lawn manicured to a perfection I've only seen in lifestyle magazines. A black Maybach with tinted windows is parked out front—this must be Rosenberg's car that Nick drives.

I'm looking forward to seeing Nick again, the memory of his handsome smile spiking my heartbeat with excitement.

More importantly, Rosenberg is on my mind right now. This is his domain. And I'm here, by some lucky circumstance, so close to meeting the man who… Right, he could potentially be dangerous, so I should probably tone down my excitement.

I park just like I was told, next to several other cars on the side of the mansion, obscured from the front by arborvitae trees. A tall man stands by the side entrance, watching me. He's dressed in a sleek dark-blue suit and crisp white shirt, despite the heat outside.

Getting out of the car, I put on a well-practiced friendly smile and walk toward him.

"Julien, is it?" I offer my hand for a shake.

He could be handsome if his expression weren't so stone-like. His hands are cupped in front of him in a bodyguard-like stance. Granted, he's built like one, broad-shouldered and intimidating. He's probably in his early thirties, a head taller than me. Close-cropped black hair and intense hazel eyes that bore into me unblinkingly.

"Julien, the house manager," he replies curtly, disregarding my outstretched hand.

Oh-kay. "I'm Natalie," I say, mirroring his stance—feet slightly apart, hands cupped in front of me. "I'm here for a job."

He doesn't move, guarding the side entrance to the house. "I need your driver's license, address, car registration, and references."

Wait, what? "Nick didn't say anything about that."

"Nick might've offered you special treatment, but I need this info for safety reasons."

Jesus, is everyone in this house so intense? And I haven't even met the boss yet.

"This job is temporary, as far as I understand," I say with a straight face. "You needed someone reliable and fast, at short notice. No paperwork was mentioned."

I give him the same cold treatment in return, silence burning between us. I don't mean to argue, but I've learned to negotiate the terms with the many employers I've had in the past. It's Thursday, and if I'm supposed to work here for only three days, skipping paperwork shouldn't be a big deal.

"When do I meet the boss?" I ask with confidence.

Not a single muscle on his face moves. "You don't. You are here to help with the party. As far as I understand," he adds, mimicking me.

His eyes still bore into me. I didn't even discuss with Nick how much I'll get paid. He said the house manager would go over it. Since this guy doesn't argue back, I think I passed the first test. I'm sure he got the instructions about my arrival, but he's trying to be difficult.

"I can start anytime," I say. Preferably, right now.

"Three days, then I'm pretty sure we won't need your services," he says, giving in, though I don't think it's up to him.

"I'll talk to Nick about that." I cock my brow at him, and his lips tighten.

It seems like Nick is the boss's favorite. If I butter him up, I might have this job for longer. I don't mind, especially if it pays under the table.

And I'm definitely meeting the boss. This guy here just doesn't know it yet. He doesn't know I couldn't care less about the party. My main agenda is the Man of the Year.

6

ANONYMOUS

Another girl. A pretty one this time.

I replay the footage of your car entering the gates, and you talking to the house manager minutes later.

You are friendly. Eager. A little too eager.

You have no idea what's waiting for you here. Your friend is fighting for her life in the hospital, but here you are—following in her footsteps, walking straight into the trap.

7

NATALIE

We still haven't moved an inch closer to the staff entrance door. I think Julien is profiling me. We have a little staring competition going on, and I let him take his time, not saying a single word, feeling the tension rising in me—I want this job badly.

"It's quite unusual," Julien finally says, "that you got this job so fast and at the request of the boss."

My eyebrows rise in surprise. "The boss? I talked to Nick, the driver."

"Makes sense."

Does it? "Meaning?"

"Special favors and all."

"No, actually..."

I shut up instantly when I realize what he's insinuating.

Are you kidding me?

It takes me a moment to pull myself back together. Julien must've noticed my expression change, because a barely noticeable smirk curls at one corner of his lips.

"Follow me," he says in a tone five degrees colder. He finally opens the staff door and—what do you know—holds it for me.

I can tell that I'm unwanted here, but once again, nothing I haven't seen before. Every business and establishment has a well-oiled crew that often doesn't warmly welcome the outsiders right away.

"Apparently, there's an issue with one of your housekeepers," I say to make a point as I step into a bright hallway.

Julien stops and stares at me again.

Ugh. If we're going to pause in every room we walk through, it will take a week to walk through this mansion.

"Make sure you follow the rules and instructions," he says, "so there's no issue with you either."

Either? Is that a warning?

"Work dress code is a black button-up," he says monotonously, as if reading a memo, "black pants, black shoes, and a white neckerchief around your neck."

For cleaning? Really? I was expecting some sort of common uniform, not dress clothes.

"No loose hair," he continues. "No perfumes, incense, or air fresheners. No food anywhere outside the staff quarters. Don't be late for work. You won't be able to leave early either, unless previously discussed." He is reciting the house rules like I'm a prisoner. "You've already met Dave. There's one more security guard, Steve."

I nod.

"The housekeeper is Rosalie. She'll be in charge of everything you do. There is a gardener, Walter, a maintenance worker, Sagar, and a driver. This"—he motions to his left—"is the staff stairs to the second floor. To my right is the staff kitchen, the storage room, and lockers."

He turns and walks toward the doorway that leads into a spacious kitchen. The large kitchen island is crowded with boxes and bags of what appear to be catering supplies.

"Well, hello," says a cheerful female voice, and I turn to see a short woman in her forties approaching me with a smile. "I'm Rosalie, the housekeeper."

She offers her hand for a shake.

Black pants, black button-up shirt with—yep—a white neckerchief around her neck. Her jet-black hair with gray streaks is tied into a knot at the back. Her smile is warm, but her gaze on me is more curious and cautious than friendly.

"Natalie," I say, shaking her hand enthusiastically. "Nice to meet you."

As with any work dynamic I've seen in the hospitality industry, Rosalie, by all obvious markers, is the binding element in this staff crew. She's probably the only one I'll like, the only one I'll really interact with, and the one who will eventually give me the scoop on anything I ask. That's what I'm hoping for.

"I'm here temporarily," I explain eagerly. "I've worked in the food and beverage sector for seven years. I'm glad to be here."

She glances at Julien, then returns her eyes to me. "We are happy to have you." Lies, but at least she tries, unlike the house manager. "Did Julien explain the rules to you?"

I intentionally ignore him. "Barely."

The side entrance door in the hallway slams shut, and a man bursts into the kitchen.

"I don't know why he wouldn't wait until morning," the man rants, seemingly frustrated. He is shorter than I am, with a thick mustache over his upper lip, dressed in—surprise, surprise—all black.

"Who?" Rosalie asks him.

He takes off his blue baseball hat and wipes his sweaty forehead with his forearm, then picks up a bottle of water from a stack on the counter and takes a few greedy gulps.

"Nick," he responds, sniffling. "I could totally fix his shower. But no, he called an outside service company at ten last night."

"I'm not surprised."

"Why would he get an outsider?" he snaps, then catches sight of me and freezes. "Who is that?"

Nice to meet you too.

It really feels like they have a close-knit circle here at The Splendors because he also looks at me like I have three eyes. I should get used to this.

"Apparently, Nick has more trust in pretty outsiders than us," Julien quips.

I'm not surprised he just poked me again. But then his words, "Pretty outsider," work their way into my brain. *Pretty.* So, he thinks I'm pretty. And he hasn't even seen me in heels and a minidress, with fake eyelashes and nails, all dolled up.

"This is Natalie," Julien explains. "She is here to help with the party."

The man furrows his brows in confusion. "She's with the catering crew?"

"Actually," I interrupt, "I'm here to replace the other housekeeper." I step toward him and offer a handshake. "Natalie."

He looks at Julien, then Rosalie, then returns his gaze to me, and his lips instantly stretch in a diplomatic, white-toothed smile under his black mustache. It's as if he's gotten a hidden cue to be friendly.

"Welcome. It's a nuthouse here, but as long as you don't

deal with the boss, you'll be fine." He shakes his head from side to side. "Also, if you need anything, repairs or whatnot, you tell me."

"Sagar is our maintenance man," Julien introduces him.

Sagar presses his palm to his chest in a theatrical bow. "That's me. Handyman. Repairman. Car guy."

"Nice to meet you," I say, puzzled by his sudden change in attitude. I like him. I also like Rosalie. I'm yet to meet Walter, the gardener, and the other security guy.

"She won't be staying for long." That, of course, comes from Julien, who seems to have the same phrase on repeat.

Rosalie gives him a reproachful glance. "Well," she says, taking a deep breath and releasing it with a long sigh. She pushes off the counter, walks up to Julien, and pats him gently on the arm. "You give her a quick tour, and then I need her for a whole bunch of things that were Darla's responsibility."

One, I bet Rosalie is the only one who's allowed to be so informal with Julien.

Two, I guess Darla is the name of the previous house-keeper, and I have a feeling that there's more to her absence than a sudden emergency leave.

Julien is already walking out, and I hurry after him. Just before turning the corner of the doorway, I look over my shoulder and see both Rosalie and Sagar staring at me. The smiles are still on their faces, but the friendliness in their eyes is gone.

8

NATALIE

"What happened to the other housekeeper?" I ask Julien when we are out of the kitchen.

"She had a seizure while intoxicated," he says, without turning, as he leads me down the staff hallway. "On the job."

"That's not good."

"No. Hence, one of the first rules in this house—absolutely no drinking. No alcohol is allowed in the house except for on special occasions and at parties. If you notice anything of the sort, you report it."

"Understood. So the boss is the only one allowed to drink?"

Julien gives me a look over his shoulder. "No. The boss doesn't drink. Because of personal history, this rule comes from him directly."

I suspect that the *personal history* is the reason the boss is engaging in some sort of self-intervention. I make a mental note to bring minis of booze to work. Meeting the boss and getting him to talk is my main goal. There's no better truth serum than alcohol.

The staff hallway opens into a spectacular two-story space. The clouds have dissolved, and the living room and hallway are bathed in the sunlight streaming inside through the floor-to-ceiling windows.

Wow! This looks like a palace.

Julien swings his forefinger in the air. "Living room." He flicks his wrist in the direction of the main door hallway. "Main entrance."

The furniture is minimal—a white living room set, an abstract painting the size of a Persian carpet on the wall. A staircase with a stainless-steel railing leads upstairs. I lift my face to study the intricate frescoes on the ceiling and a silver honeycomb chandelier.

"Second rule," Julien says, already walking in the direction of an archway leading into the east wing of the ground floor. "No phones."

I almost skip, trying to catch up with him. "Pardon me?"

"No phones are allowed at work." He doesn't look at me, just keeps walking. "When you arrive for work, you lock your personal belongings in the locker in the staff room. That includes your phone."

"Why?"

"Conference room." He motions to an open door that we pass so quickly that I don't get a chance to look in. "Mr. Rosenberg works with sensitive information," Julien continues, without stopping, in the same monotonous voice that annoys me. "His business depends on extreme discretion. If you had proper training and qualifications, you wouldn't be asking these questions."

I don't bother responding. I will definitely try to dig into the *sensitive information*. That's what I'm here for.

"Library," Julien blurts out, motioning to yet another door without stopping. "Lounge," he says next.

This time, I slow down and peek into the half-open door. The lounge could pass as a club, with modern red leather banquettes and armchairs, glass coffee tables, a grand piano, and a freaking DJ stage.

"Are you coming?" Julien says louder, demanding my attention and watching me with poorly concealed annoyance.

I hurry toward him.

"This is Mr. Rosenberg's office." Julien points to a closed door as we continue walking. "Rosalie is in charge of cleaning it. You are not to go there unless she specifically tells you to."

"No problem."

I make a mental note to make Mr. Rosenberg's office my priority. Right after Rosalie. I have to be in her good graces. Though Julien is the house manager, I'm sure he has better things to do than watch me at all times.

"Do I need to sign a non-disclosure agreement?" I joke, then realize that the permanent staff probably have to.

Julien doesn't respond to that question, just looks down at me. "You clean the main rooms during the assigned time slots. You are not to go into any rooms that are not assigned to you, unless the other housekeeper says so."

"That's intense."

"We work around Mr. Rosenberg's schedule and to his convenience. Not the other way around."

The Pentagon sounds less intense than this mansion. And there are more rules to come.

"You are not to touch personal belongings," Julien continues as we walk. "That includes clothes, paperwork, anything that's not food or drinks."

"What about laundry?"

"Rosalie handles that. You are here for cleaning and

cleaning only. As well as handling the cleaning for the other staff members."

I raise a brow. "Pardon me?"

"The kitchen and lounge area at the back of the house—we take our breaks there. You will be responsible for cleaning that area, dishes, trash, and so on."

So, I'm the cleaning lady for the staff—that's a downgrade.

"You will do everything Rosalie tells you to do. The main focus is the coming party this weekend. Don't forget, you're a temp."

We'll see. It takes all my willpower not to bite back with a snarky comment.

There's a gym and a theater at the far end of the mansion, but we turn around and walk back through the living room and hallway toward the staff area. To my disappointment, there's no sign of Geoffrey Rosenberg or Nick.

"Are there any rooms I should avoid when Mr. Rosenberg is at home?" I ask Julien.

"Rosalie will curate your schedule."

"I mean, right now? Are we disturbing Mr. Rosenberg?"

"He is out."

Damn it. I need to be more alert about when the boss is home or not.

I spot Rosalie at the far end of the living room, dusting the paintings. She smiles at me, and I give her a tiny wave back.

She likes me. I'll make sure she *loves* me and trusts me with cleaning the rooms that Mr. Serious here told me are off limits.

We are about to walk into the staff hallway when I look back at her. Rosalie's not dusting anymore. She stands still and watches us, her smile gone.

Odd. Maybe not so friendly after all. Maybe she's not dusting but following us.

The staff stairs take us to the second floor.

"So we don't use the main staircase?" I muse.

"No," Julien says curtly.

He is a man of few words. Getting him to talk is like pulling teeth.

"Is anyone besides the owner allowed to walk the house as they please?" I ask.

"Nick is," he replies curtly.

Sounds like Nick has access to pretty much anything. If I were to guess, Nick is Rosenberg's pet, and I just so happen to be on great terms with him.

"Master bedroom." Julien points at the closed door and keeps walking.

"Aren't you going to show it to me?" I ask, but he ignores me.

"Guest bedroom." He motions toward yet another door. "Guest bedroom and a bathroom. Another one." He doesn't bother showing them to me.

I'm almost trotting after him. His stride is wide, and the house tour is too rushed, as if I'm wasting his time, and he wants to get it over with, which is probably the case.

I take in the paintings on the walls, the sculptures, and art pieces here and there. There are no pictures of family or friends. No mess. No personal items.

There are seven bedrooms in the house but all in all over twenty rooms—I lost track. Why would one person need such a big house for himself?

My eyes drift upward, to the hallway ceiling and the light fixtures.

That's when I see it—a camera—and my stomach twists in unease.

9

NATALIE

"There's a camera here?" I point to it in the corner of the ceiling.

"There are multiple cameras inside the house, in the main areas," Julien says, unfazed. "There are several cameras outside."

I tense up and lower my eyes. No matter where you are, cameras make an average person nervous. They project a not-so-subtle sense of invading one's privacy. Nowadays, cameras are everywhere—on the streets, in public places, inside businesses, at every other traffic light. We never give it a second thought. But there's something unsettling about being watched on cameras in someone's house and in a private setting.

Julien points to several more rooms and then shows me the upper-floor balcony that's larger than my entire apartment in Jersey City. Before I even get a chance to poke my head outside, he's already walking back to the staff stairs.

"Who's watching the cameras?" I ask as we descend the

stairs, and I notice another camera. I make a mental note about its location.

Julien tugs at his suit sleeve, not sparing even a glance in my direction. Seriously, it's impossible to have more disregard for a fellow staff member. I respect discipline, but come on! A tad of politeness never killed anybody. I have a strong feeling we won't be getting along.

"Some of the catering supplies will be here at noon tomorrow," he tells me. "I expect you to be here at ten."

"In the morning?"

He halts abruptly, making me run into the side of his arm, and slowly turns to look at me. He cups his hands in front of him in that bodyguard pose that makes him look intimidating. Especially when his eyes bore into me.

I don't budge and raise my chin.

"You wanted a job? You got a job," he says. "Work hours at The Splendors are nonnegotiable. You can walk out right now."

Somehow, I feel that he'd like that.

"What are the hours tomorrow?"

"Ten to eleven."

"And on Saturday?" I hope I can survive this guy and the brutal hours.

"Ten to eleven. However, if you are asked to stay later, you are expected to do so. That's why you get paid in cash."

That's a thirteen-hour day two days in a row, plus however many hours they want me to work today. No wonder the other housekeeper got intoxicated on the job. On second thought, I need to find out what exactly happened to her. Emergency leave and intoxication on the job are two completely different things. The stories about her don't line up.

Julien is studying my face like he's expecting me to

change my mind. "If it's too much, tell me right now. No hard feelings."

He already said that.

"No, thank you." I give him my most insincere smile, holding it in place.

Our eyes lock. This is a staring competition again, and this moment between us is peculiar. I'm tense and nervous, but also excited. Why? Not sure. I didn't expect to run into a guy who would be challenging me before I even started my job. Also, trying to talk me out of it.

But it's all right. He's easier than 50 percent of the customers I've dealt with while bartending since my sophomore year in college. In Manhattan, that's no small achievement. I need to find a proper angle with him.

"You think you can follow the rules?" Julien asks.

He's definitely good at what he does. Discipline, order, meticulousness. All about the rules.

I can do it too. Definitely. For the money, but more importantly, to figure out why Rosenberg's house feels like a prison and what happens to women here.

"Absolutely," I say, still holding my smile, though my face feels numb.

Julien studies me a bit longer. A barely audible "hmm" escapes him.

"Ready to start?" he asks.

Well, goddamn, ask me again.

I bring the tip of my right hand to the side of my forehead in a military salute. "Yes, boss."

For a moment, Julien's gaze softens, and the skin in the corners of his eyes crinkles in a teeny-tiny sign of a smile, which never makes it to his lips.

"Did you bring a change of clothes?" he asks.

I shake my head. Not a big deal, right? It's my first day. I'm thinking they'll have me organize the kitchen, count the silverware and glassware, decorate the party room. Despite the catering service, there's still a lot of work to do.

My phone pings, and by reflex, I pull it out of the pocket and see a message from Nick.

Nick: How is it going, doll?

I can't wait to chat with him. Maybe he'll give me pointers on how to deal with this grumpy house manager.

"Your phone has to go into the locker," Julien reminds me in his cold-as-steel voice.

His eyes are on my phone screen. He slowly blinks up, his gaze on me hardening.

"Right," I blurt, tucking the phone into my pocket. "What do you want me to start with for the party?"

He turns and starts walking away, throwing over his shoulder, "You start with cleaning all the bathrooms."

Asshole.

10

ANONYMOUS

Welcome to The Splendors Mansion. Did you know you'd be watched? No. And here you are, in a gilded cage, as we speak.

You're careful, playing naive. Way over your head, though you've yet to realize that.

I can tell you're used to working with people. You're good with the staff. You don't like being told what to do, especially when your superior is a man who isn't falling for your charms, but you handle it well.

Pretty, too. Observant. While you're given a tour, you study everything with the diligence of a spy.

You think you know what you're doing. I'd say, "Good for you," but that won't work at The Splendors.

And then you spot the first camera.

For a second, your expression stiffens. You look straight at me from the screen. I rewatch this part several times—the look of surprise on your face is priceless.

You drop your gaze and ask about the camera.

Does it bother you that you're being watched? I'll be watching you at all times. I'll know your every step.

The Splendors Mansion is a trap. This place swallows people and spits them out—all chewed up. Or dead.

You shouldn't have come here, Na-ta-lie.

11

NATALIE

Eight bathrooms, five guest rooms, and hours of steam-mopping later, I'm finally done with my first day of work.

I've learned from the experience that service people are grossly underestimated. Too bad. It's your sober bartender who hears all your drunk conversations and accidentally spilled secrets. It's your waiter, who's used to reading faces and noticing body language, who knows exactly how your date feels about you. Your taxi driver hears every conversation you have. And your cleaning lady knows all your nasty habits. She also takes out your trash, but you have no idea that some of the secrets you throw out don't necessarily disappear into a landfill.

I haven't found anything incriminating in the house yet. Geoffrey Rosenberg and Nick have been gone all day, which is disappointing, but I have at least two more days to investigate.

It's eight in the evening, and the mansion is quiet. I put the cleaning supplies into the utility closet and approach the staff kitchen.

The hushed voices there make me stop short just outside the kitchen entrance.

"She's in a life-threatening condition," the soft male voice says, Julien's.

"How serious is it?" Rosalie asks.

"No brain activity. I don't think she will survive."

My heart thuds with panic. Cara? Are they talking about Cara?

Prolonged silence is followed by a sigh and more silence.

The detective's words at the hospital come back to me. *There's another young woman in this very hospital in a similar condition...*

Maybe they're talking about Darla, the housekeeper.

"She can only blame herself," Rosalie says. "She should've stayed away from him."

"That's not the point," Julien argues. "The point is that someone got hurt, on *my* watch, Rosalie. This job is supposed to be safe."

"Not in this house."

"Yes. In *this* house. The rules are simple. As long as everyone *follows* the rules."

"She broke the rules, Julien!" Rosalie snaps in a strained whisper.

"I know! And now I feel responsible."

I hear a thud, like someone hit a surface with a dull object or a fist.

"Listen, Julien, you can't blame yourself for someone getting involved with a dangerous person. Darla broke the rules. She should've stayed away from Rosenberg." So, they *are* talking about the housekeeper. "She knew about the consequences. It's not your fault. Not mine either. Not anyone's."

"A person. Got. Hurt, Rosalie," comes Julien's angry whisper. "*Again.*"

Suddenly, everything goes quiet, so quiet that I know what that means—they heard me or sensed me.

Crap.

I can't get caught, absolutely not, so I walk through the doorway and into the kitchen, pretending to pick at my nails, and run right into Julien's hard chest.

"Excuse me," I say, feigning surprise as I stare up into his intense hazel eyes. I shift my gaze to Rosalie. "Is everything okay?" I ask, acting innocent.

They don't answer, so I throw a careless glance at my nails, making a point of bringing them closer for inspection, as if that's the most important thing in the world right now.

"I'm done," I say casually and step around Julien toward Rosalie. "What's up with you two? Something happened?"

Rosalie exchanges glances with Julien, who stands behind me.

"Nothing, sweetie," she lies. "Just talking."

I can feel Julien's burning gaze. I don't turn. If he could burn me with his stare, I'd be engulfed in flames.

He stomps out. The staff entrance door opens and closes, and I meet Rosalie's eyes. "Is he okay?"

She rolls her lips in. "He's fine. Just upset. Don't mind him. He's a good guy. He's just..."

"Doesn't know how to be friendly?" I prompt.

She chuckles.

Uh-huh. The number of times I've heard, "He's not an asshole, he just has a lot on his plate right now," probably tops the list of most-used excuses for assholes.

I get Rosalie to casually chat for a minute, asking her about the house, other rules, and what we'll be doing for the party as I plant off-topic questions in between—about other employees, our boss, and the company he has.

Rosalie is stingy with replies, but I get useful bits here and there. I was right—besides being a driver, Nick is Rosenberg's assistant and, apparently, his lackey, though Rosalie calls him an old-fashioned "butler."

I bring up Julien's words about special favors. "Julien and Nick don't get along?"

She trains her hard stare on me. "A pretty girl like you? You should keep your head down in a place like this."

"What do my looks have to do with anything?" I press on. Her words make me wonder what Darla looked like.

Rosalie's friendliness vanishes in seconds. She starts rearranging boxes of party supplies on the kitchen island.

"Stay away from the boss and his business," she says, her movements jerky and irritated. "I'll see you tomorrow at ten in the morning. Don't be late. Wear the right attire."

Well, there's that.

She walks out abruptly, leaving me by myself. Julien is nowhere to be seen. I'm grateful and surprised that he's not escorting me out of the house to make sure I don't steal anything. He seems like that type of guy.

Right now, the house is a giant ghost town. I grab my purse out of the locker and check my phone. There's a missed phone call from my friend Tess. A number of text messages from other people. Everyone is freaking out about Cara, asking what happened. I don't have an answer to that. *Yet.*

Before leaving, I tiptoe toward the living room, wanting to sneak a look around.

From what I've learned cleaning the bathrooms and staff area, the cameras are in the main hallway, living room, upstairs hallway, the staff staircase, the back terrace, and two more cameras around the property. I kept a mental note of the house plan. When I get home, I will do a sketch of the mansion as well as the location of the cameras and try to calculate several pathways through the house to avoid them.

I am about to step into the living room when Rosalie's voice behind me makes me jump out of my skin.

"You looking for someone, sweetie?"

She stands in the middle of the staff hallway, her unblinking stare on me.

Heart pounding, I feign a cheerful expression. "I was just looking for Julien. Have a question for him." I can tell my lie didn't fly.

"I can pass on the question. What is it?"

I wave her off. "Regarding the paycheck. I'll ask him tomorrow." I smile, walking past her. "Have a good night, Rosalie."

"You too, sweetie. And, Natalie?"

I turn and meet her cold stare.

"It's in your best interest not to snoop around in this house."

I nod and walk away. I don't hear a single sound behind me. That means Rosalie hasn't moved, and she's watching me.

12

NATALIE

The air outside is hot. The sky is dark, but the lights around The Splendors illuminate the mansion and garden in a magical way. In many fairy tales, horrible things happen in pretty castles. Just saying.

Nick hasn't responded to my texts. Bummer. I have a feeling I won't be seeing him much.

Muffled voices come from some distance away. As I walk to my car, I squint at the structure about forty or so yards away—a garden shed. As I approach my car, the voices go quiet, but I can discern two figures by the shed and smoke in the air. It's Sagar, the maintenance guy, and probably the gardener I haven't met yet. Both are staring at me from a distance.

Tomorrow, I will make a point of introducing myself to the gardener. Maybe he's friendlier than the house manager. I'll get to Julien, I promise myself. I'm good at establishing work connections.

I turn on the car, roll down the windows, and, while driving toward the gate, let out a heavy sigh—one day down.

When the entrance gate doesn't open to let me out, I honk and squint at the booth but don't see the guard. I honk again, and this time, the gate starts opening, revealing an unfamiliar guard on the other side.

"C'mon-c'mon-c'mon!" He motions frantically with his arms. "Move it!"

I assume this is the other security guy, Steve. When I pass the gate, I see Dave on the sidewalk outside the fence in a struggle with a man.

Interesting.

I pull over to the curb to see what's going on.

"I said move!" Steve barks at me from ten feet away.

I'm in no hurry and very curious, so I stick my head out the window. "Is everything all right?"

"I will tell the police!" the man shouts as Dave punches him in the face.

"Yeah, wow," I say, watching the two from a distance. "Why *don't* you call the police?"

Steve stomps toward my car, scowling and motioning at me again. "Young lady, I said, *move!*"

Rude!

Suddenly, there's a pained yelp, and I see Dave curled up on the ground. The stranger runs across the road ahead of me. "Tell Rosenberg he needs to talk to me!" he yells as he stops at a safe distance. "Or I will tell the police what he did!"

Dave scrambles to his feet and makes a move in his direction, but the man starts running away, up the sidewalk, and disappears into the darkness.

Steve leans into my open window, his face twisting with anger. "Which part of 'move' don't you understand? Nothing to see here. Come on!" He angrily motions for me to leave.

Oh, gee, Team We-Suck-At-Our-Job.

"Good night," I say with a fake smile.

As I drive off, intentionally slowly, I frantically search the side of the road. When I finally see the guy peeking from around the thick bushes just a little ahead, I slow down even more. It's dark here at night, in the suburbs, but I see his face clearly in my headlights. His eyes lock with mine as I pass him. I stare at the rearview mirror, and just before the night swallows his silhouette, I see a quick flash in his hands—I'm pretty sure he just took a picture of my car.

I don't know what the fight was about, but the security guards were in no hurry to call the police on him. Odd, to say the least.

Only now do I notice that my heart is racing as the stranger's words ring clearly in my head.

"I will tell the police what he did."

DAY 2

13

NATALIE

Trixy the Rat throws suspicious leers at me when I check myself out in the living room mirror.

It's six in the morning, Friday. At my previous job, this would've been one of the busiest days of the week and most profitable when it comes to tips. The job of a housekeeper is humbling, but I don't remember the last time I was so uneasy about my job.

My uniform is definitely uptight. Black dress pants, black slip-on shoes, a black button-up, plus the stupid white neckerchief that I bought at a dollar store. My dark hair is neatly swept back into a tight ponytail, loose strands secured by hairpins. Minimal makeup.

Before leaving, I clean out my purse, and a card falls out:

Detective Lesley Dupin,
Jersey City Police Department.

I wonder if I should give her a call, tell her what I'm up to. But she might want to start investigating, show up at The Splendors, mention me or Cara. That would be a disaster.

I decide against it. Also, I probably shouldn't be carrying a detective's card in my purse while I'm at The Splendors. I drop it on the table, but just in case, I punch the detective's number into my phone and save it under "Dupin."

"Keep an eye on things," I tell Trixy the Rat and leave my apartment.

I stop by the local bakery around the corner and get blueberry muffins, Cara's favorite. It's a silly thing to do, considering Cara is in a coma. As I drive to the hospital, the delicious smell spreads through the car, jolting back memories of our routine mornings. It makes the lump in my throat grow bigger, my eyes burning with tears.

She'll make it. She'll make it. She'll make it.

"No progress," the nurse says when I walk into Cara's hospital room. "Oh, and those…" Her brows knit together in pity as she looks at the box of muffins in my hand. "They are not—"

"I know," I cut her off softly. "I'll just leave them by her bed for a bit. Please don't get rid of them right away. It's breakfast time. These are her favorite." I smile apologetically. "I know, it's silly. It's just…" I'm ready to burst into tears as I look at the motionless Cara, surrounded by tubes and monitors, while I'm talking about stupid muffins.

The nurse nods in understanding, and as soon as she leaves the room, I set the box of muffins on the small table by Cara's bed and force a smile onto my face.

"Hey," I say. "How are you, babe?"

It's so heart-wrenching—talking to her in a coma, pointlessly smiling. After what happened to Lindsey, I prayed I'd never hear those awful sounds again—the beeping of the heart monitor and the hissing of the ventilator.

My chest tightens. A sob breaks free.

Oh, god, I'm going to cry. No, I'm not. I'm not going to cry. I won't.

I take a deep breath and hold it to stop the tears, but they are already spilling down my cheeks.

"It'll be fine," I murmur between sobs and rush out of the room, unable to be there any longer, feeling angry that I can't handle this well, and helpless, so utterly helpless.

I'm sorry, I repeat in my mind. For being so weak. For being alive while one of my friends is dead, and the other one is close to it.

It's all because of *him*. I need to meet Geoffrey Rosenberg. I should use my looks to get his attention. There's a downside to being attractive—yes, there is such a thing. I found that out by bartending in fancy places and having to say no to the drunk advances of men who think that their wealth gives them unlimited power. Occasionally, it backfired. At one of my jobs, an arrogant drunk accused me of serving him cheap booze and siphoning the expensive one just to get back at me for rejecting his advances.

What I heard at the mansion yesterday is a much darker story. Apparently, Darla, the previous housekeeper, got too close to Rosenberg and got hurt. She might not make it. That's worse than getting fired. That sounds like…a murder attempt.

Maybe that's what that shady guy who got into a fight with security last night was alluding to. Maybe he's Darla's relative? I doubt anyone will tell me his name.

I did sit down last night and draw a simple plan of the mansion as I remembered it. I marked the cameras that I noticed—six in total. That gave me several ways to move around the mansion through the staff quarters with minimal notice. We'll see how that works out.

The sky is gray. It rained all night, and it's still drizzling, but it's supposed to be sunny later on. The radio is blaring in my car as I'm driving to work. The talk-show host goes on and on about crypto stocks spiking in the last two days.

"Money, money, money, money," he rants. "We love to hate it, but we can't live without it."

"Money doesn't make one happy," a caller says, an older woman who begins spewing seasoned wisdom about life.

The host interrupts her. "Clearly, you never had any. It's not the money that matters but its *quantity.*" He laughs triumphantly.

The caller starts arguing, and I kill the radio. They are both right and wrong.

As I pull up to the gate of The Splendors Mansion, Dave opens it and gives me an unwelcome stare through the booth window.

Dude, get over it.

During the half-hour ride from the hospital, my mood has done a full 180. I'm determined to find out what my rich boss is up to.

I roll down the window as I pull up beside the security booth. "Rough night?"

He doesn't answer.

"Next time this happens, maybe call the actual professionals to handle it? Law enforcement or something?"

I can see anger boiling in him, and I drive into The Splendors with my signature work smile. By the time I finish working here, my face will hurt from fake smiling.

The buzz of the lawnmower is coming from behind the

house. I'm not an expert, but I'm pretty sure no one ever mows wet grass. This whole place is out of whack.

I park and walk into the house.

The mansion is eerily silent, like a tomb. I put my purse in the locker and check the staff kitchen.

"Hi!" I say, getting a nod from Rosalie, who's hustling with boxes and crates of delivered catering supplies. I don't understand why the catering company doesn't just take care of everything. But then, I'm not one to make recommendations on how to handle business in the house of a man whose privacy is ensured by a mile-long list of NDAs and security checks.

Julien is nowhere to be seen, which makes me relax a bit—I already prepared myself for a day of marching to his war drum.

I didn't see the black Maybach at the front either, which means Rosenberg and Nick are gone. Again. I haven't even gotten a glimpse of my new boss yet.

"Let's get to it," Rosalie says, interrupting my thoughts.

The agenda for the first half of the day is to sort out the party supplies, silverware, and decorate the back terrace later. This gives me an opportunity to chat Rosalie up.

"Have you done this all your life?" I ask, meaning this type of job.

"Not quite," she responds.

Rosalie comes across as humble, but there's a certain authoritativeness about her. I would picture her doing something completely different. Maybe working at the Department of Motor Vehicles, with that calm attitude and impassive expression. She could be a 911 operator. Maybe even a parole officer. Yes, Rosalie could definitely be a parole officer, one of those who gives you a piss jar to collect your urine for a drug test, does it with a no-nonsense face, and actually watches you in the process to make sure you don't cheat.

She is definitely a listener. Almost every one of my questions gets avoided and redirected back at me.

"You grew up around here?" I ask.

"No," Rosalie answers. "You don't look like a local either. Not a city girl. Not a Jersey one. Where are you from?"

Just like that, every attempt of mine to get her to talk about herself only points back at me.

Not even an hour goes by before Julien walks in.

Hello, Officer. "Good morning," I say, overly cheerful.

He scans me, then grabs an apple from a fruit basket and loudly bites into it. "The boss is home," he murmurs under his breath.

Just like that, Rosalie's expression turns blank.

Loud voices come from the main hallway, and the door slams shut somewhere at the front of the house.

"Is that Mr. Rosenberg?" I ask, apparently talking to a wall, because no one responds. I glance between Julien and Rosalie, neither of whom meet my eyes.

This is probably the first workspace I've been to where all the staff look like they'd rather be anywhere but here. And that's a bad sign.

14

NATALIE

I'm anxious to meet Rosenberg, excited and petrified at the same time. I need to see for myself if the predator looks like a predator in real life. If he is one, that is—I might be getting ahead of myself.

The staff entrance door opens, and a tall man walks into the staff kitchen. He's in his forties, with shaggy brown hair, glasses, a sweaty face, and black clothes. I take it this is Walter, the gardener.

Startled at seeing me, he stops and gives me a prolonged, hostile stare that kills any desire to introduce myself. He literally turns his back on me and leans in toward Rosalie.

"Another opportunist?" he asks, knowing perfectly well that I can hear him.

Well, hello to you too.

"The boss is home," Rosalie says, and the gardener's expression freezes for a second. His Adam's apple bobs as he swallows hard.

Why is everyone suddenly so uptight and self-aware?

He clears his throat. "What additional lights do we need on the back terrace for the party?" he asks, his eyes shifting from Rosalie to Julien to me.

Julien slowly chews, studying the apple in his hand like it helps him think better. "The illuminated spheres. Follow the setup chart that the landscape designer sent. Also, the table-top fire pits need to be tested."

The gardener listens but doesn't move his eyes off me—the tension in his glare is real. Meanwhile, I try to focus on the voices in the main hallway. Two of them. The soft one belongs to Nick. The other one, louder and lower, is sort of booming, but in a soothing way, and belongs to Rosenberg, I assume.

In a minute, Nick walks into the kitchen, his gait confident, his expression cheerful. He looks sharp in his suit pants and crisp white shirt, unbuttoned at the neck, the tie loosened.

He stops short, noticing our small gathering. His eyes immediately fix on me, the corners of his lips tilting in a smile. "How is it going?"

His smile looks almost illegal among the sour faces of the others.

"Great," I lie. I don't carry on the conversation. Mr. Warden here might just fine me for fraternizing.

"Hey, guys, boss wants Thai," Nick says to no one in particular. "The usual. Make it for two people."

According to what I learned from Rosalie, Geoffrey Rosenberg spends a significant amount of time in his home office. He doesn't like home-cooked food, so the kitchen is hardly ever used. Instead, he orders takeout and apparently loves international cuisine.

Rosalie nods and fishes a phone out of her pocket. Oh? So, she's allowed to use a phone, but not me? Unfair.

"It should be about forty minutes for the delivery," she states, typing away.

"He also wants those coconut drinks he had a week ago," Nick adds.

"I'll have to go get them from the shopping plaza."

"Have Natalie go."

Rosalie stiffens at the words and glances up at me.

Supposedly, Rosenberg is known for having sudden and unusual whims for food and other things. Like hákarl, Icelandic fermented shark. Or some trending gadget he sees online, something he wants "now, within an hour," so someone has to drive and find it at a store. Eccentric, but not unusual, considering his wealth and resources.

Anyway, I'm in. Driving is much more relaxing than scrubbing floors or sorting party supplies.

Nick scans everyone in the kitchen until his eyes stop on Julien. "Have Natalie bring it to the office when it's ready."

I lower my head, gloating at Julien's reaction, which I can't see, but I can totally picture well-disguised irritation and sparks coming out of his eyes when he looks at me.

Rosalie tries to argue. "*I* can do it."

Nick scrunches up his brows apologetically. "Boss wants to meet the new staff member."

I glance at Nick, who purses his lips and walks out, leaving the awkward silence behind him.

This shouldn't be a big deal, but the silence in the kitchen feels hostile.

"You heard him," Julien finally says curtly to no one in particular. "Make it fast," he snaps and walks out too.

So, that's that—the boss wants to meet me. That's good, right?

Walter glares at me, shakes his head, and leaves.

Rosalie stares at me like I just stole her husband. Her tone is sharper than usual. "You are quick. I hope it works out for you."

The bitterness in her voice is unmistakable. This whole weird scenario has one conclusion—apparently, Geoffrey Rosenberg likes young women around. Darla, Cara—those are just a few I know whose interactions with him have put them in the hospital. But that's because they didn't know they were playing with fire, right? I do. And I know how to play by the rules.

15

NATALIE

Welcome to the lion's den!

Nick opens the door to let me into the office, and I step in, balancing a tray with food.

The spacious room is almost empty. A Persian carpet. An oversized artificial bonsai tree in the corner. At the far end of the room, armchairs and a coffee table are arranged in a semi-circle in front of a massive mahogany desk and a leather chair. Behind them, there's a giant painting of ultramarine water and a tiny goldfish in the very center. There's no other furniture in the room, which makes the walk along the stone-like walls to the desk feel ceremonial, as if I've come to a meeting with a king. I'm assuming this intimidating design is intentional.

The Man of the Year is even more handsome in person.

Geoffrey Rosenberg stands by the side of the desk, his hands in his trouser pockets as he studies the painting on the wall in deep contemplation. It gives me a chance to place the tray on a small coffee table while I observe him.

He's tall, with neatly combed red hair and a short-trimmed beard, in stylish contrast with his mint-colored dress shirt. He is silent and motionless yet somehow emanates power and confidence. A Manhattan, Van Winkle, and Cartier man. Definitely a bourbon guy. Maybe cognac.

"Boss?" Nick prompts.

Rosenberg slowly turns in place, his gaze instantly locking on to me.

I straighten like a soldier.

For a second, my heart does a panicking thud—after all, I was with Cara when they hooked up at the club. I didn't pay much attention to him that night, just another fancy-suit-and-expensive-watch-Wall-Street-type. Also, I looked different—my hair loose and styled, a minidress, high heels, and tons of makeup. It was dark. Hopefully, he was intoxicated enough not to remember me, and I pray to God that Cara never mentioned my name.

"This is Natalie, the new housekeeper," Nick says, tilting his head toward me.

Rosenberg doesn't bother approaching, doesn't even take his hands out of his pockets. "Natalia?" His investor-friendly voice is low and rich, authoritative, and could probably sell snow in Alaska. "Sounds Russian."

He gives me a thorough up-and-down, which makes me uneasy.

"It's Natalie," I correct him.

"Hmm." He assesses me with lazy curiosity. "Natalia fits you better."

Asshole. I've met many versions of Rosenberg when I tended bar in Manhattan, learned to deal with them, but right now I need to play the part.

There are all sorts of meaningful eye contact. The most

powerful flirty one is not batting your eyelashes, no. It's intense and unblinking. It seems almost inappropriate, as if you are caught off guard by the other person's charm. Doe eyes with a hint of surprise, as if you've just met your soulmate.

I learned that one from Cara. She's an expert. She can be cocky, playful, shy, brazen—depending on the guy and the situation. And let me tell you, she has a knack for profiling rich men down to a science. But this particular gaze— she taught me, even gave me a training session, "Just in case. Never know who you need to schmooze"—catches most men by surprise.

That's how I look at Geoffrey Rosenberg right now. Once his eyes meet mine, he blinks away for a second and then returns his gaze to me, as if for a double take, and I'm working, working, working that gaze like my life depends on it.

A man like him is probably accustomed to the advances of women who are hunting for wealthy beaus. But he might not be used to genuine infatuation, or what he thinks genuine is.

He lifts his hand to his face and rubs his chin, keeping eye contact with me.

"Boss?" Nick prompts again.

For Nick, this is awkward silence. For me, it's a guarantee that the next time Rosenberg sees me around, he'll remember who I am.

"It's nice to meet you, Mr. Rosenberg," I say in my sweetest voice, though my body is so tense that my spine could crack at a touch.

Rosenberg finally looks away. "You should be a model," he says absently, his attention back on the ridiculous painting of a goldfish.

I turn to Nick, who flicks his eyebrows.

"Anything else?" I ask him.

He looks expectantly at Rosenberg, who doesn't bother to respond.

Nick shrugs and smiles at me. "Thanks."

Before I close the door on the way out, I hear Rosenberg's voice. "She's pretty."

This should be a compliment.

Then why do the hairs on the back of my neck stand on end?

16

ANONYMOUS

I know what you are doing, pretty girl. Look at you, two days in, and you've graduated from flirting with the staff to batting your lashes at your new boss.

I rewind the footage of you in the office, zoom in on your face, and study it. Your gaze is electric. Well practiced. It's not the same as it is in person, but it still gives me goose bumps.

And you are smart, so smart, working the people around you with caution, unlike many other women before you.

I like smart. But this? This is the wrong game for you to play, Natalie.

17

NATALIE

"Thank you for letting me meet the boss," I say to Nick as we stand outside the staff entrance during a lunch break.

"No problem," he says. His tie is gone, the sleeves of his shirt are rolled up, and he slowly twirls a set of keys around his fingers. "He usually doesn't bother talking to the staff. He must've noticed you, though. I don't blame him."

I like compliments. Except when they come from a possible serial predator like Rosenberg.

"I wish Julien were as friendly as you," I say.

Nick instantly tenses. "Julien is very protective of his workspace. The boss likes him."

"Do *you*?"

He chuckles. "He's all right. Why?"

"No, just… He doesn't like me much. No one does around here."

"Sure they do!" Nick clicks his tongue in protest. "They are just trying to get a sense of what you're like. It's normal. You are smart. And nice. What's not to like?"

I chuckle. "Thanks."

His gaze on me softens. "Thank you for being here. It's refreshing."

"Refreshing?"

"Well, everyone is pretty uptight here. It's nice to see a new face. A beautiful one, too."

I think I blush. Nick casts his eyes down, a smile lingering on his lips. He's quite irresistible.

"It can get"—he pauses for a moment—"stressful here, you know." He glances up at me. "Boss can be demanding. Sometimes, pretty intense. Occasionally, he... I'm just glad to see a friendly face here, though I don't get to very often."

He's cute. The younger version of him would have been labeled a "golden boy." I'm sure women are all over him. But I have a feeling he has little to no time for a personal life.

"Listen," he says, concerned, "if anyone mistreats you, let me know, and I'll pass the word to the boss. Honestly, you are doing Julien and his team a favor by helping."

"It's all right."

Nick nods repeatedly. "This job is easier than saving lives, you know."

I frown, then realize he's making a joke about the day we met and instantly burst into laughter. "Right."

His boyish grin, along with the cute tilt of his head, instantly cheers me up. I wish we could hang out more. If everyone in this house were like him, this would've been an ideal job. Besides scrubbing bathrooms, of course.

"Wanna get together tonight?" he asks, his gaze on me somewhat hesitant.

Ah, there it is. I knew this was coming. Nick is a good catch. Charming, kind, considerate. I could probably get some background on Rosenberg from Nick if I played my cards right. No fraternizing is a rule at any workplace. But I'm sure, if I wanted to, I could hook up with Nick, and he'd make this slide past the rules and the boss. Do I need this right now?

The detective's warning sounds more sinister now. Maybe I should reconsider my dating rules. What happened to Cara makes me want to run a background check on everyone.

Nick's gaze on me is hopeful—he knows I'm evaluating him, and he wants to hear a yes.

For a second, I consider a date with him. If Nick lives in the city, it might be easier to bail out if the date goes wrong. I go out, I don't like it, I split. I'll just have to come up with a valid excuse so there's no tension at work.

"Where do you live?" I ask, mulling over the options.

Nick tilts his head at some spot vaguely behind him. "Right there."

I don't get it. "Right there where?"

He points to the small structure behind the mansion. "The guest house."

"Really? *There?*"

"Yeah." He looks down and kicks the gravel with the tip of his fancy shoe. "The boss requested that I move closer to him. He's needy." Nick chuckles. "He also has a tendency to request me at odd times, in the middle of the night and whatnot."

"Do you even have days off?"

Nick shrugs. "Not really."

"Wow, that's tough."

"That's life. I get paid well, and I need money. Just like you."

"Things we do for money, huh?" I joke, wondering if I ever imagined, while working three jobs and putting myself through college, that I'd be cleaning toilets in a mansion at the age of twenty-seven.

"Yeah, so, I can't invite you in," Nick says apologetically, and I almost feel bad for him. "My place is not fancy, to say the least. Plus, it's on the premises. Believe it or not, the boss keeps a close eye on things. I wouldn't want…"

Nick pauses as if trying to choose the right words, then scratches his eyebrow with his forefinger, still twirling the keys in his other hand. There's something awkward about it, as if he's nervous or trying not to reveal too much.

"It's… Yeah, I like to take my personal life outside this place," he says. "To get away from here as much as possible, you know?"

He starts twirling the keys between his fingers faster. He looks almost slightly embarrassed, or uneasy, or…scared? I can't figure it out. But he avoids meeting my eyes, and there's no trace of humor on his face.

Rosenberg's right-hand man doesn't like being at The Splendors? This is another red flag.

"So what do you say?" Nick's hopeful smile is suddenly back.

I feel like Nick is desperately trying to get away from this place, if only for an evening. Any other time, I'd jump at the opportunity.

But that's a no. I don't know what his schedule is like, but I'm doing a thirteen-hour workday and thirteen more hours tomorrow. There's a high possibility of me cleaning up after the party on Sunday. That's aside from driving to the hospital every morning to see Cara. The last thing I can think about is a romantic evening. I definitely shouldn't get involved with anyone around here.

A key chain among the other keys in Nick's hand catches

my attention—it's a tiny souvenir Empire State Building with a spire.

I nod toward it, trying to divert the topic. "Sentimental?"

Nick chuckles, giving it a glance. "I love New York City."

"Where are you originally from?"

"*Not* the city," he says quietly.

He must be a small-town guy who was lucky to score an important job. I sort of see why he's trying so hard to be nice to everyone. Both Cara and I are from a small town. Me—from a dysfunctional family. Cara—from an abusive one. Despite having lived in the big city for nine years and having graduated from college, we still struggle to make a decent income and feel like outsiders on a daily basis.

"Yeah, the city is great," I say, then turn to the house, giving it a backward nod. "Especially when you have this kind of money."

"Everyone's dream, isn't it?"

"Wouldn't you want to have a place like this to yourself?"

Nick's smile takes on a disappointed tilt. "Wouldn't *you*?"

"Something is off about this place," I say, baiting him.

Judging by how Nick's expression falls, my words struck a chord. "How do you mean?"

"I don't know. Just... Rules. Cameras."

He clears his throat. "Listen, our boss is an important man. He will be a billionaire soon. We all get paid very well, so we play by the rules and wag our tails because we need these jobs."

There's something suspicious about the work energy in this place. Everyone seems a bit too serious, and when Rosenberg is around, everyone steels their spines like they are afraid of him.

"Do you know what happened to Darla?" I ask.

And here it is again—Nick's expression freezes, the keys silent in his hand.

"She…she got tied up with the boss," he replies, tonguing his cheek.

"Tied up how?"

Nick looks away, reluctant to talk. The secrecy surrounding Darla is becoming annoying.

The staff door squeaks open, and Rosalie's head pokes out. "Need you here," she says, motioning for me to come inside. I guess my break is over.

I exchange knowing glances with Nick.

"Mr. Warden must be requesting me," I joke. "Let's talk later? Maybe hang out?" I say to give him hope and reluctantly get back inside the house.

Rosalie doesn't look at me as I step into the kitchen. I can tell she's annoyed. She doesn't hide her emotions well.

"You should try harder to be more professional," Rosalie says.

I want to snort but hold it back not to anger her. "And I'm not?"

"Our boss doesn't like when the staff is fraternizing."

"Isn't Nick his favorite?"

"Yeah, well, to a point."

"What do you mean?"

"Anything suspicious, and you will be in trouble."

Oh, gee, here comes that warning again. "Having a friendly talk with a staff member is suspicious?"

"Gossips are. Especially anything that has to do with the boss."

"Is that what happened to Darla?" I bait her.

Rosalie flinches, then stares me dead in the eyes. "She talked too much. Just like you."

18

NATALIE

Nick enters the kitchen, interrupting our chat.

"Boss and I are leaving," he announces, then walks out, his whistling echoing in the hallway.

"We have some cleaning to do on the ground floor while they are gone," Rosalie says curtly. "The library needs to be vacuumed and dusted."

"Again?"

I'm positive that it had been done several days ago as per the schedule Rosalie showed me on my first day. She only cocks a brow with a silent warning.

"Sure," I say obediently and go to the utility closet.

"Gloves!" Rosalie reminds me.

That's another rule—mandatory nitrile gloves when cleaning the house. God forbid I leave a single fingerprint or a smudge behind!

Ugh.

I want to be angry about Rosalie monitoring me at all times, including during my lunch breaks. I know what I'm doing. But I need to be on my best behavior, so I tuck my pride away and head for the library, dragging the vacuum cleaner and a basket with dusting supplies.

At least I get a chance to explore a new room in this mansion.

The library is impressive. All the books are in perfect order, perfect color, perfect size. It's like those fake bookends that you see in movies. Catching myself thinking that, I actually pull a book off a shelf to make sure it's real. As I do, the entire row of them, light as a feather, pulls back.

They *are* fake!

I snort in amusement and look around the room with its floor-to-ceiling bookcases along two opposite walls and a comfy chair in the center. If this is all fake, then why make a library at all?

It's none of my business, I remind myself. Maybe Rosenberg has good taste in food but doesn't read. Maybe he only reads numbers. Maybe only on his computer. Who knows?

I start dusting the bookshelves, and only a minute goes by before something catches my attention. It's an empty McDonald's cup tucked between the bookcases.

"So much for being an international cuisine connoisseur," I murmur as I pick it up, about to throw it into the trash bag, when a familiar smell catches my attention.

Working as a bartender for years makes your nose attuned to the smell of alcohol. How strong it is. What kind. The label. The quality.

Slowly, I bring the cup to my nose.

Oh, man. It's booze, all right. I pop the plastic top off and sniff it properly—whiskey, it's definitely whiskey.

An amused "huh" escapes my lips.

So, Rosenberg is not a cognac or bourbon guy after all.

I toss the cup into the garbage bag and ponder what this means. There's a strict rule of no booze in the house. A rule enforced by our boss. A rule that everyone follows so as not to jeopardize their jobs. If the staff wanted to drink at work, they'd do it in the staff area, and there are plenty of places to hide booze there. So this is not the staff's doing. There haven't been any visitors since I started working here either. This leaves me with a very obvious conclusion—Mr. Rosenberg, the genius behind IxResearch, is a closet drunk.

There's nothing funny about a person's addiction, but we are talking about a potential predator. I just found something I can use against him. I make a mental note to buy a bottle of Johnnie Walker Blue and keep it hidden in my car, in case it comes in handy.

I keep dusting. I've never been a fanatic about cleaning, but in the last two days, I've realized that dusting is the worst, second only to scrubbing toilets. I have bristle dusters, cloths, a feather duster, an air bulb, cotton swabs, and that doesn't begin to name the multiple cleaning solutions. This place doesn't have any dust, I swear, yet I'm pretty sure Rosalie goes around with a white glove and drags her forefinger along every surface for traces of dirt.

So I keep diligently dusting.

Art is the worst. I don't know which pieces are extremely expensive, so I treat them all like they are priceless. Including the stupid spider-looking flower with big gaudy rubies on its branches that stick out of the wall in different directions. Annoyed, I swipe my feather duster a little harder.

That's when one of the red stones pops off and falls to the floor.

My breath hitches in my throat. I stare in panic as it rolls off, and then something else happens—it snaps into two pieces.

No! No-no-no-no!

I get on my knees, reaching for it with my fingers, and freeze.

I'm not an expert, but I have a pretty good idea of what I'm staring at. I'm not paranoid, and I'm not making this up, because the tiny object that has separated from the art piece is definitely a camera.

"Oh, crap."

Instantly, fear steals the air out of my lungs. I pull my hand away and stare at the object, then get on all fours and bring my face closer, my nose almost touching the floor.

My first thought is that this room is supposed to be camera-free, so clearly, this is a hidden camera.

My next thought is that this might be one of many.

The next thought makes my stomach drop—whoever is watching this camera will see that I was the one who knocked it off and discovered what it was.

The thought that follows is—who can I tell? Does anyone know? What if they do, and I blabber about it, only to get myself in trouble? What if they don't, and I end up getting *everyone* in trouble? What if I'm already in trouble, and I end up like Cara? Or Darla?

My thoughts race a mile a minute, my heart beating so hard in my chest that I think I'm having a panic attack.

"Think," I tell myself, still on all fours like a dog sniffing the ground.

I lean just a little bit closer and study the camera piece. It's a small black square, about an inch across, with a round lens and some sort of goo behind it—probably the adhesive that held it in place. The camera sits on its side, the lens pointing away from me.

Okay, good. That means that I haven't stared directly at

the camera yet, which means I still have a chance of acting oblivious to it. That is, if there aren't other cameras watching me right now.

Maybe not everything is lost yet.

Holding my breath as if it will blow the camera away, I retreat on all fours away from it, then slowly rise to my feet.

Okay. Okay. I got this.

I take a deep breath, put the duster away, pick up the vacuum cleaner, and plug it in. Keeping my eyes on the floor, I turn it on and start vacuuming the carpet. I purposefully vacuum a distance away from the little eye on the floor but in its direct view. I force the vacuum in front of the camera, knowing exactly where it is but never looking in its direction. After thoroughly vacuuming in front of it, I swallow hard, take in a deep breath, and run the vacuum over the red stone, then over the camera piece on the floor.

As soon as they are sucked in with a horrible crackling sound, I close my eyes and exhale, taking my time to catch my breath as the vacuum keeps going. I'm playing dumb and hoping that it works.

I did it. It's all good. It will work out.

At this point, I wonder if I should walk out of this mansion and never come back. If anything else suspicious comes along, I will ask for my pay and do just that.

But there's a party tomorrow. I need money. And I need to get any damning information possible on Rosenberg.

One more day, I tell myself. Those who fall victim rarely know the predators they are dealing with. I do. What's the worst that can happen?

19

ANONYMOUS

I stare at the dead feed from the library's camera, then rewind the footage.

Of course it's you.

You are not a cleaning lady, but I already know that. You are a nuisance. You should be fired before you stick your nose any further in my business. But that might create a problem too.

I zoom in to rewatch the footage at the exact moment the hidden camera from the art piece in the library hits the floor.

At first, all I see is the carpet. Then you step into view, vacuuming, not looking at the camera. Slowly, your feet on the carpet come close to the camera. The vacuum follows. Then—poof!—the feed goes dark.

I feel a prickle of irritation.

This better be a coincidence, Natalie. Or your sloppiness. Pray that you didn't actually notice the hidden camera or tell anyone about it. If you did, then we have a big problem.

20

NATALIE

Here's the breakdown.

Two days at The Splendors—it's a weird place, to put it mildly.

Scrubbing floors, toilets, cleaning the staff area—not my thing, but I've done worse jobs in my life.

Cameras everywhere, plus the hidden ones no one told me about—god knows how many of those there are and for what reason. Don't underestimate my paranoia when I use the bathroom.

A millionaire boss who likes "meeting pretty female staff"—creepy.

Strict privacy rules, no cell phone—that I can deal with, but, again, creepy.

Gloves on almost all the time—my hands are starting to itch already.

A stalker and security personnel who, for some reason, avoid the police—a warning.

A half-dead former housekeeper, whose position I'm filling in—mega red flag.

What did I miss?

A smart person would've run from this place. I should. I could call up Rocco and pick up a shift or two on the slowest days at his Irish pub to make some cash.

But this job is all about persistence.

Yeah, Mom used to call me strong-headed. My former boss called me the Iron Lady. Customers called me tough. Cara just says I'm stubborn. Personally, I think I have an issue with letting go of things. I don't like leaving things unaccomplished. I don't give in to other people's crappy ideas and suggestions. Abrasive power only makes me rebel. The phrase "You can't" only makes me try harder. I like rules and discipline and hate when people think of themselves above them. I've dealt with plenty of wealthy folks who think that rules are meant for those who can't buy their way out of them.

They are not wrong, and I hate it.

That's the thing with Rosenberg. He is a perfect example of living in a world where money can bypass laws, morals, and ethics. The police can't do anything about it. The law is made for the masses, the 90 percent of us.

Me? I'm just a stubborn girl. But as one smart man said, "Do not underestimate the power of a mosquito."

I'm sure unlawful things are going on in this house. I'm also pretty sure Rosenberg is responsible for the girls in the hospital. I will get enough dirt on him to cause a stir. I will take it to bloggers, journalists, or whoever is willing to listen. I want Rosenberg to catch on fire, and not in a good way.

I just need to find something incriminating first.

Hence, I still work at The Splendors, dealing with all

the red flags. Including the current one—I think someone is following me.

It's eleven at night, and I'm driving home, pulling off the highway at the exit to Jersey City, when I notice the headlights of an SUV behind me. That SUV has been following me pretty much since I left the mansion.

At this point, my paranoia is ramping up. I catch myself nervously tapping my finger on the steering wheel, my eyes constantly checking the rearview mirror.

It's late, but Jersey City has traffic, though undoubtedly not nearly as much as during the day. Still, I manage to lose the SUV behind me. I drive for several blocks around my apartment building, looking for parking while making sure I really lost that SUV. I turn down the radio volume, like that's going to help me find a parking spot or solve the mysterious SUV riddle.

When I finally find parking, I get out of the car and sprint toward my building, punch the entrance code, and hurry down the hallway toward my apartment. I pretty much fall inside, slam the door, and press my back to it, exhaling in relief.

It's a relief that one more day is over. That I have a job. That I'm good, no money, but there are worse things in life than being poor. I could be broken. I could be—

My eyes catch sight of the photograph in the living room, the one of Cara, Lindsey, and me in Atlantic City, on the beach, several years ago, right before Lindsey passed.

"My two favorite things," Cara used to say. "The ocean and you babes."

My heart does this strange thing where it halts for several seconds before starting to beat faster, and suddenly my chest feels like it's being filled with liquid tar.

It's hard to breathe. The emptiness of the apartment claws at me like a monster.

"Me too, babe. Me too," I whisper.

I pull my phone out of my purse and check the missed calls.

I'm Cara's emergency contact, her "sister," and if there had been any change to her condition, they would've called me. But there are no missed calls from the hospital. That means there are no updates.

Tears prickle my eyes. I never really liked this apartment, but Cara made it come alive. We needed that change after Lindsey's passing, after we moved out of the quirky ware-house loft the three of us used to rent in Manhattan. We struggled to come to terms with Lindsey being gone, and right now, I feel just like I did for months after Lindsey's funeral, when the world carried on as usual while I felt like I lived in a depressing hellhole of sad memories.

I take deep breaths, trying to snap out of my miserable mood. The emptiness of the messy apartment is suffocating. Usually, when I came home, there would be jazz music blast-ing from Cara's room at the same time as some popular pod-cast would blare from the computer, while she'd be dancing, cooking in the kitchen, several costume projects scattered on the couch, the coffee table, the floor. And amid all that, she'd probably be on the phone, too, while trying to give me a spoonful of whatever new dish she was cooking. Or there would be someone sitting on the couch, drinking, someone "dirt-poor but extremely talented" or "a star on the rise" or one of the many people Cara made friends with anywhere she went in the city. That's my Cara.

But no, this apartment is silent, eerily so, the only sound being that of Trixy scratching at the cage.

"Wait up, girl, I'll feed you," I tell her, pushing away the depressing thoughts. I'm kicking off my shoes when my eyes land on a note on the floor—someone must've slipped it under the door.

I pick it up.

It's handwritten on a restaurant napkin.

You don't know what you got yourself into.
Rosenberg is dangerous.
Call me ASAP.

There's a phone number scribbled beneath the words.

My pulse starts racing. This is the proof I've been waiting for—Rosenberg is a criminal.

But that's not why my knees go weak.

Someone knows where I live, and that someone came here.

21

NATALIE

Whoever left the note has been very quick to track me. Technically, with a little more digging, they could've gotten my number too. I check the missed calls on my phone, but none of them are from unknown numbers.

So I dial the one on the napkin.

After one ring, I hear a low male voice. "Hello?"

"Hello?" I reply, my heart pounding like a drum.

"Who is this?" The voice sounds harsher this time.

"I got your note with the phone number on it."

"Natalie?"

A shiver runs through me at the sound of my name from a stranger.

"Who is this? And what do you want?" I ask sharply.

"Where are you calling from?"

"My phone."

"God dammit! Seriously?"

"What's the—"

"They might be listening."

"Who?"

"Your boss, that's who," the man snaps. "Or someone who works for him."

I swallow hard. "Is this some kind of joke?"

"Did anyone touch your phone?"

Wait, what? I don't know why I'm having this conversation with a stranger, but he keeps asking questions.

"At The Splendors," the man says angrily, "did anyone *touch* it?"

"What do you mean, *touch*? What is this about?"

"I mean what I mean. Did you ever leave your phone unattended?"

"It's in the locker when I'm at work."

"God dammit!" There's a loud rustle on the other end of the line. "I need you to call me back from someone else's phone. Right now. It's in your best interest."

Before I have a chance to ask him more questions, the line goes dead, and I stare at my phone like it's a ticking bomb. Slowly, I turn it in my hand and inspect the phone case to see if it might've been tampered with. How would I know if there was a bug in it? I don't have a password lock on my phone, so technically, anyone could've gotten into it when it was in the locker at the mansion.

Now I'm paranoid. I've only worked at that place for two days, and already someone is stalking me.

But this is exactly what I was looking for. This stalker—hopefully not a psycho—might have something on Rosenberg. At least there is someone else besides me who thinks that Rosenberg has secrets the police would love to find out about.

I knock on my neighbor's door. Lilly is a nurse. I don't know her too well, and people have stopped knocking on neighbors' doors to borrow sugar or a screwdriver. These days, most people are suspicious about any sort of request from strangers, but one thing everyone can relate to is technology.

Lilly's wary face appears in the open door. "Hey, what's up?"

"Hey, girl. Listen, I'm sorry to bother you. My phone started updating and then got stuck, and I need to make a quick phone call to my employer." I scrunch up my nose. "Can I borrow your phone for a sec? It's a quick one."

"Sure!" She laughs.

Like I said, there's a mutual understanding that we can't function without technology these days.

I fake a friendly laugh in response. "This is one of those scenarios where I wish we still had landlines in apartments like our parents did."

"No kidding." Lilly unlocks her phone and passes it to me.

"I'll be quick!" I wait for her to step into the other room, then I dial the number from the note.

"Yes?" the stranger rasps on the other end.

"It's me again. Calling from my neighbor's. Better?"

"Yes." He doesn't catch my sarcasm. "So, you are the new girl at The Splendors. I guess you know what you're doing."

I silently gasp at the words. He definitely watches the mansion since he knows I'm new there.

"Who are you?" I demand.

"We met briefly when security threw me out the other day."

Aha! I was right. He's the man I saw outside the gate, in the dark, just a day ago. He might be dangerous. But! There's also a possibility that he has some dirt on Rosenberg.

"I only have a second," I snap. "Tell me what this is about."

"I know you think you are clever, but you won't be able to pull it off yourself."

"Pull off what?"

"Listen to me. We can take that asshole down together."

I'm pretty sure I know the answer, but I need another confirmation. "Who?"

"Rosenberg."

Right, taking down a famous millionaire sounds like a piece of cake. But I'm curious. "You need to tell me more."

"Yeah. I'm trying to get to him, but that seems impossible."

"I only met him once."

"Yeah, well, you work in his fortress. I need you to pass on some information."

"Didn't you say he's dangerous?"

"If you are smart, you'll do it in such a way that you won't get caught. I have information that will land him in prison. But I can't reach him. You are the girl on the inside, and I'll pay you if you do what I tell you."

Huh. This is interesting, but it also sounds like it might get me in more trouble than I need. "You said he is dangerous, so why—"

"Listen, this is not a phone conversation. We need to meet. Soon. Before you end up like everyone else."

My jaw drops. "Excuse me?"

"I'll get in touch again. Don't call me from your phone. Use someone else's or a burner."

The line goes dead.

DAY 3

22

NATALIE

For most people, a party in a million-dollar mansion is a fun event. For service people, it's the toughest day of the week.

For me? Well, this is probably my biggest opportunity to observe Geoffrey Rosenberg. There will be a hundred or so guests. People will be getting drunk. Meanwhile, I'll get a chance to eavesdrop. I'm not the only one who thinks Rosenberg is dangerous. That's confirmed. Good.

Play by the rules, I remind myself. *Act normal.*

That's definitely tricky, considering there are more cameras in the house than what I was told about.

It's Saturday. I'm up at sunrise. Despite my mind reeling with the thoughts about what this day is going to be like, I need to get to the hospital to see Cara.

The first stop is the local bakery. Today's special is champagne-and-strawberry muffins. Cara is a muffin connoisseur. She would have spent her last dollar on this flavor. So I spend mine instead.

Next stop is the hospital.

"No news," the nurse says.

Yeah, yeah. I ignore her.

"You'll make it, babe," I tell Cara as I set the box down on the side table. I take out one muffin and sit down in the chair by the bed. I don't have much time, but I need to be here for at least a minute, to remind myself why I need to go back to The Splendors.

"Remember the fig-and-goat-cheese artisanal muffins you once bought?" I ask Cara as I take a bite of the muffin. It's delicious. "You said they smelled like goat diarrhea. Even Trixy refused to eat them."

I smile to myself, taking another bite of the muffin. I won't cry this time.

When I finish the muffin and leave, the room smells vaguely of strawberries. I hope that wakes Cara up. Silly, of course, but I'll come here every day until she wakes up and recovers.

Powered up for the day, I drive to The Splendors.

The level of luxury at the mansion is just another reminder that money can cover up a lot of crime.

"Not this time, Rosenberg," I say to myself when I step into the staff kitchen, ready to start the day. Maybe it's wishful thinking, though I'm hoping for a self-fulfilling prophecy.

As soon as Rosalie gets me to help her wrap the silverware, I start a subtle interrogation. There's got to be a way to get someone to explain the strange things around here.

"Do you know how many cameras are in the house?" I ask Rosalie.

She doesn't respond, doesn't look at me as she continues to methodically sort the silverware.

"I found a hidden one in the library," I say cautiously.

That's when she stiffens, panic flashing across her face,

if only for a second. Slowly, she raises her eyes to me, her expression already rearranged into the usual professional mask.

But that momentary panic of hers is contagious, creeping down my spine. I realize that I might have just made a mistake. Have I?

Rosalie's eyes dart to the door as if she's making sure no one else is around, then return to me. "Did you tell anyone?"

On reflex, I look over my shoulder at the door too. "Should I?" I ask in a hushed whisper, stepping closer to her. "So you know about it? How many cameras are there?"

Rosalie passes me the napkins for the silverware. "That's what happened to Darla," she says quietly, the words seemingly harmless but making my blood go cold. "She was in way over her head, careless, despite the rules."

Jesus Christ! What is it about this house and the rules?

"Do me a favor, sweetie," Rosalie whispers, stepping closer to me, her eyes locking with mine again. "Not a word about it to anyone. Understood?"

"Does anyone know? Besides you?"

She swallows hard, blood draining from her face.

"Natalie, listen to me," she says more harshly. "I know how it sounds, and you can still walk out of here any moment, but you *cannot*—please, sweetie, for your own good—you *cannot* mention this to anyone. This"—she motions with her forefinger between her and me—"is where it ends. Right here. *Now.* No one else should know that you know."

"What about Julien?"

"*Not* Julien. *Not* Nick. *No one*, Natalie, you hear me?"

"What's going on in this house, Rosalie? I need to know. It's Rosenberg, isn't it?"

At the mention of him, Rosalie's face acquires an almost

sinister expression, and she hisses with a hostile tone I haven't heard from her yet, "Don't be stupid, Natalie."

She closes her eyes, almost as if in pain. When she opens them, they are misted with tears, and her lips stretch in a smile that's far from genuine and therefore feels out of place. The change is so abrupt that it catches me by surprise. She holds her palm in front of her, as if stopping me, and I notice that she's trembling.

"Please, Natalie," she pleads. "Either leave or be very quiet about anything you see here." Her eyes search mine for confirmation, then she turns away. "I can't do this anymore. I can't," she murmurs.

I don't understand what that means, but I realize one thing—Rosalie is not irritated with me. She's really afraid of something.

23

ANONYMOUS

That's sweet, Rosalie, but I know why you want to keep it a secret. If you tell on Natalie, she might become a liability. You, in turn, will end up with nothing—no money, no job, and very lucky to still be alive.

This is a catch-22.

You are a good woman, Rosalie, but even good people often end up in the worst situations. That's why you are here. That's why you follow the rules, even though you're scared out of your mind. So, so scared, I know. You are hoping to come out of this on the other side unharmed and a winner.

Except Natalie is crossing the line. Tsk, tsk. This is a complication.

From now on, you will be very *careful, Rosalie. Remember what your husband had to go through years ago? Remember the pain? The anger? His suicide note? Your hate so pitch-black and blinding that you wanted to set the world on fire?*

Exactly.

Head down, and do your job.

24

NATALIE

Mr. Warden walks in, causing Rosalie to stiffen, as if she has just been caught stealing.

In addition to his never-changing suit and tie, Julien has an earpiece in his ear and a little push-to-talk mic clipped to the edge of his lapel. They are all serious about this party.

His eyes slowly rake over me, then Rosalie. "How is everything?"

Shouldn't he be concerned about other things? Like the catering company? The terrace setup? Security?

"What is the house manager's job exactly?" I ask, diverting his attention from Rosalie, who is as quiet as a mouse, avoiding looking at him, which weirds me out. Is she afraid of him?

Julien tilts his head to one side, his expression unchanged as he studies me. "Making sure you do yours."

"I am, boss." I give him a military salute.

Rosalie snorts, glancing between us.

Julien stares at me with a straight face, not a muscle moving. He's immune to my jokes.

Mimicking him, I make a serious face and study him in turn. "This must be awful. I can't believe they are doing this to you," I say in a grave voice.

His eyes narrow just slightly. "Excuse me?"

For a moment, I tease him with silence. "This part of your job contract. It's cruel."

There's confusion in his hazel eyes that soften just a tiny bit. "Which part?"

I nod in pretend concern. "Not allowed to smile on your job."

His expression freezes just as Rosalie bursts out laughing.

I can't help grinning, holding his gaze that changes with realization. He sucks in his cheeks.

"It must be pure torture," I taunt him.

"She got you, Julien. Got you good." Rosalie cackles with laughter, and I swear, Julien's jaw tics as he tries really hard to hold his composure.

"Don't you have something to do?" he says in a deliberately cold voice as he fixes his suit jacket, already on the way out.

"Sir, yes, sir," I shout at his back and wink at Rosalie.

"He needs that," Rosalie says quietly. She stands at the counter, aimlessly rubbing her fingertips, eyes cast down, all serious again.

"Needs what?"

"Someone to make him smile."

I snort. "No kidding."

"He's having a rough time."

"Rough time how?"

She ignores me.

"Okay, Rosalie, you can't do that." I set my hands on my hips and duck my head, trying to get her to look at me.

"Rough how? Because I can say that about dozens of people." Including Cara. Rough doesn't even come close to describing her state right now. Clearly, Darla is way beyond that.

Rosalie sighs heavily. "He is dedicated to this job, but he is having a hard time with it."

"Doesn't seem like it."

"He's good at keeping himself to himself. But Mr. Rosenberg... Well, let's just say he is not exactly a model gentleman when it comes to people. Women, especially."

And here comes the first proof of what I think the true Rosenberg is. I step closer to Rosalie. "I heard a story or two," I lie.

Her eyes dart at me. "From who?"

"Nick."

She frowns. "Really? What did you hear?"

I can't tell her about Cara, and she won't tell me about the former housekeeper, so I have to lie in order to get her to talk.

"Let's just say, I heard that women who get close to Rosenberg end up not in a good way."

I hold her stare until she finally breaks off. "Nick told you that?"

I don't answer so as not to lie again. I want her to talk.

She purses her lips. "I suggest you stay away from Rosenberg."

"Is that what happened to the previous housekeeper? She didn't?"

Rosalie's expression hardens, but she doesn't reply.

"What about Nick?" I press on. "Should I stay away from him too?"

I can tell she doesn't like what I'm saying.

"How about all the other men in this household? Julien? Walter? Sagar?"

She shakes her head, closing her eyes. "You are trouble, aren't you?"

Her hand goes to her chest, and she rubs the pendant hanging off her neck as if in meditation. Her eyes are closed, her lips slightly trembling.

I didn't mean to make her upset or angry. I probably do come across as snappy—courtesy of my previous jobs. Rosalie seems like a nice person, maybe the only one here who somewhat cares about me.

"Who's the pendant from?" I ask softly, trying to divert the topic.

Her eyes are still closed. I think she's having a moment.

"My husband," she replies in a whisper.

"You love him?"

Her eyes snap open, and I see them glistening with tears. "He's dead."

I swallow hard. "I'm sorry, Rosalie. I didn't mean to be a pain in the butt. Just… Nick did me a big favor by helping me out with this job. I'm grateful." I step up to her and give her a big hug. She doesn't hug me back, but that doesn't matter. "And I like working with you. I'll be on my best behavior, I swear."

"That's what Darla said," Rosalie murmurs barely audibly, but I hear it. "Before she was poisoned," Rosalie adds, making my blood run cold.

25

ANONYMOUS

Tsk, tsk. Rosalie just can't help but talk, talk, talk. What is the first rule in this house? Keep your mouth shut. But no, now she has to bring up Julien.

What Julien needs right now is to focus on his job. Right, Julien?

I rewind the camera feed and zoom in to see the way you look at Natalie.

I know you so well. I know that look, Julien. One girl is all it might take for your downfall.

The model citizen, Julien Lenz. Perfect credit score. Brilliant record. Excellent work ethic. House manager. Owner of Precision Staff Management Company.

Liar.

This house is full of liars and spies. You, Julien, have more secrets than anybody. Everyone trusts you. You are in charge of this house. And what do you do? Fixate on a pretty stranger you met just three days ago.

She's trouble. She's nosy. She's spying. She's lying. And you know that. She can ruin everything you've worked for. There's already enough collateral damage. People have been hurt. She might be next. So tuck your attraction away and focus.

26

NATALIE

At noon, the catering staff arrives—six men of various ages, all dressed in black dress pants and button-ups. Signature white neckerchiefs are in place. Seriously? They don't introduce themselves and don't talk, though they do listen to Rosalie's orders and set up tables, flowers, and minimal but elegant decor and serving stations at the back terrace and garden with the speed of lightning.

An hour later, a van pulls up to the staff entrance with a food and drinks delivery. Sagar, the maintenance guy, is the driver.

"Is this part of your job, too?" I ask him as he carries crates and cases of soft drinks, water, and liquor into the staff kitchen.

He shrugs. "I do what I'm told."

Don't we all?

I follow Rosalie's orders, casually asking at some point why the boss didn't hire dozens of people to deal with this.

"Privacy. Non-disclosure."

I widen my eyes at her. "You mean the catering staff signs a non-disclosure?"

"No. However, they are professionals accustomed to working with high-profile clients. That's the majority of the guest list."

Oh, wow. Now I'm really curious.

"Let me wait on the guests," I ask Rosalie.

"I'll need you back here," she responds, all business.

"I'm good at it," I beg her. "I've been bartending for years. Trust me, I'll be efficient and watch out for anything the guests or the boss need. Please-please-please?"

"We'll see," she replies.

When I hear the music outside, excitement spikes through me. It's five o'clock when Rosalie sends me to the terrace to do the final check.

The terrace is decorated with flowers and lanterns. The garden in front of it is dotted with tables, chairs, and tabletop fire pits. A long buffet table with fruits and desserts is set at the far end.

The main addition to the terrace is a large portable movie screen as big as those at the old drive-in theaters. There's no sound, but footage of cutting-edge technology and product demonstrations loops on the screen, showcasing augmented reality real estate concepts and a futuristic interface. Digital tablet stands are set up along the perimeter of the lawn. Rosalie was right—this is not your average party.

There are no guests yet, but several catering staff members already stand like statues, motionless, with trays balancing in one hand. Rosalie said that several others are at the main entrance.

Julien walks out onto the terrace but doesn't spare me a glance. His eyes scan the setup. He seems nervous, though nothing gives it away except for the fact that he ignores me—that's definitely an indicator. He absently adjusts the cuff of his suit sleeve almost on repeat.

"Is everything all right?" I ask him.

His eyes slowly shift from the screen to the catering staff, the tables, and the digital stands.

"Let's hope that this party goes off without any incidents," he says without looking at me.

I don't ask why this is a concern.

I tug at the annoying neckerchief and square my shoulders. "It's going to be fine, Julien."

I walk back into the mansion, hoping that this party goes up in flames.

27

NATALIE

I see why white neckerchiefs are a must for the staff.

It's six in the evening, and the terrace is crowded with guests. A lot of them wear black—black suits, black shirts, black dresses, black T-shirts, black baseball hats, and black jeans. Black is the new black again. Most people are dressed informally, and most of them are younger than me or around my age. Many look like college students.

"Entrepreneurs," Rosalie explains. "The tech crowd. Silicon Valley and all."

Not sure she understands what she's talking about, but I get it.

I sneak outside through the staff entrance to take a peek at the front of the mansion. I spot groups of guys wearing worn-out jeans and shirts that have seen better days, unshaved, young. There are more luxury cars and limos parked at the front than I've seen at a car expo. Unlike any luxury car expo, this parking lot is infested with bodyguards. Today, The Splendors is secured better than the Louvre.

Within half an hour, things get hectic. The catering staff run in and out between the staff quarters and the terrace. Sagar is helping. Even Walter, the unfriendly gardener, is here, carrying more boxed beverages out of the walk-in cooler in the storage room. Mind you, there's no food served, only fruit and desserts. These guests didn't come here to eat.

Eventually, Rosalie gives me a tray with soft bubbly drinks in champagne glasses.

"Craft cocktails. No alcohol. Go-go-go," she hurries me, and I hustle into the hallway.

I'm about to turn toward the open double doors that lead onto the back terrace when I catch a glimpse of a familiar figure in the hallway across the living room—Geoffrey Rosenberg, slipping into the library.

What would he be doing there when he has guests to entertain?

I turn on my heel and follow. I approach the door and, without knocking, gently pull at the handle. If there's a time to be unapologetically nosy, it's now.

The library is dimly lit, the only glow coming from the antique desk lamp. Rosenberg stands near the mahogany bookshelf, his back to me. I watch, my breath shallow.

He tugs at a row of faux books, reaches behind them, and pulls out a to-go McDonald's cup. He sips through the straw right there, greedily, not moving, not sitting down. There's only one thing men can be that thirsty for—booze. I should know—my dad is a prime example.

My stomach twists. It feels wrong, watching him, like it always is when you discover people's shameful secrets. Rosenberg's shoulders loosen just slightly—I know a fix when I see one. For a moment, I almost feel bad for him, then remember why I'm here.

A creak beneath my foot gives me away. Startled, Rosenberg spins around and glares at me.

"I'm sorry," I apologize, keeping my voice soft. I step into the library with a tray in my hand and close the door behind me. "I thought one of the guests was sneaking in here, and we had instructions to make sure no one does. For your privacy, sir."

His jaw tics, a flicker of annoyance crossing his face. He cracks his neck, then tilts his head toward the door. "It's all right. You can go."

Not a chance.

Steeling my spine, I approach, conjuring an obedient smile, my eyes on the cup. "I can take that…"

Rosenberg pulls it toward him. "That's okay."

"It looks almost empty, sir. I can refill it for you," I say, reaching for the cup.

The speed with which Rosenberg yanks it away from me is hilarious. In fact, he's so quick that he bangs his elbow against the shelf, and the plastic lid with a straw pops off his cup, dropping to the floor.

The smell hits me instantly—rich and sharp. Whiskey. Not even diluted.

I sniff the air, making sure Rosenberg notices.

He inhales sharply, his eyes on my nostrils as anger flashes across his eyes.

"I'll clean this up, sir," I murmur nervously. "I'm sorry. It's all my fault."

His mouth tightens. "It's fine," he grits out.

"No worries, sir. I'll take care of this," I say as I kneel beside him, set the tray down, pick up the lid and straw, and dab at the floor with a napkin.

My kneeling is intentional. I don't want him to be angry, I want him in charge. More than that—I need his trust.

I look up and catch his gaze as he assesses the lower part of my body. To be precise, my butt. He catches me looking at him, and his gaze locks with mine.

I know this gaze, the intensity, the silent question, *"Is this what I think it is?"* The seconds of doubt—even powerful men have those, calculating, figuring out pros and cons, whether to go for an opportunity or not to bother.

That's Rosenberg right now. I turn my gaze to the floor, cleaning at his feet, while he's probably trying to figure out how much he can get and what he can get away with.

"It's okay," I murmur with a reassuring smile as I get up and gently take the cup from him. "Anything you want, sir?"

He narrows his eyes on me, and I wait, my heart pounding so loudly that I'm afraid he can hear it.

"Would you like a refill?" I offer.

No booze for the boss—that's the rule in the house. Well, screw rules. This guy needs to loosen up and let that monster inside him out of the cage.

"I'm here to help, sir," I repeat.

Predators like obedience and weakness. I can see that in him, and I know what I'm doing. He thinks he knows what I'm offering. His gaze slowly slides down my body, then crawls up, making me shiver in disgust.

I cock a brow in question, with the most obliging expression I can muster, waiting for him to make a decision. Or maybe he's calculating if this is a good time to make a move.

"Hmm." His hum is low and dangerous, the meaning behind it even more so. Slowly, he steps away from me.

"I'm good." He walks past me and toward the door. "Keep this between us."

"Yes, sir."

He is about to walk out the door when I stop him. "Sir?"

He turns, his sharp annoyed gaze on me. "If you ever need anything, let me know."

"Are you with the catering company?"

Apparently, he doesn't remember me after all.

"No, sir. I'm a temp for the previous housekeeper."

Recognition crosses his face. "That's right. Natalia."

It's Natalie. But I don't correct him. Asshole will forget about it tomorrow.

"I know I'm supposed to do what the other staff tell me to do," I say in my most timid voice, "but this is your house, and your comfort is my priority. So if you ever need anything, any requests, I'm here for you."

He gives me another slow once-over. Not sure if that's a hint of what he needs from pretty women, but he's not getting it. That doesn't mean that I don't want him to think that he can.

He nods and walks out.

I raise my chin in satisfaction. I just became an accomplice in one of his little secrets. It's not much, but it gets me closer to him. Little by little, I'll find out all his secrets. I just hope I can keep myself in check, because right now, my knees are weak, and as I pick the tray up off the floor, my hands are trembling.

28

NATALIE

When I walk out onto the terrace, I spot Geoffrey Rosenberg right away. He stands at the front of the crowd, and everyone's eyes are on the giant screen.

A woman in an elegant white suit picks up a microphone and sashays toward the screen, which is now brightly lit with the IxResearch logo.

"I'm very excited that all of you are here!" she announces, gracefully smiling at the crowd gathered in a semi-circle in front of her. "At this beautiful house, with none other than the Man of the Year himself, Geoffrey Rosenberg, the CEO of IxResearch and the mastermind behind the most successful cryptocurrency exchange."

The crowd applauds. The older men and women in suits and dresses raise their champagne glasses. The younger guests in casual clothes whistle and clap with their hands raised above their heads.

The crowd slightly parts around Rosenberg, like he's Jesus, all eyes on him. He's acting cool, like he didn't just slam a cupful of straight whiskey. He presses his palm to his heart, bowing gracefully with a slightly condescending half smile.

"You all know," the woman continues as the screen changes to stock market graphs, "that IxResearch is set to go public in two days! Which means this will be an unprecedented"—she ticks her chin up—"most powerful"—she surveys the crowd with pride—"exchange venture in the history of crypto!"

The crowd bursts into more applause, mixed with whistles.

A couple of faces in the crowd are familiar—I've seen them on TV. There's a guy who owns a popular social media platform. Another one just made a splash in politics.

I thought it would be a party for the almighty figures of the digital world. And it very well might be. But it looks like the almighty are a generation in their twenties. That makes me feel old. It also makes me feel like a loser, working bartending jobs while these guys rake in millions. The Scarecrow's line comes to mind. "If only I had a brain."

The woman keeps talking as I scan the gathering and spot Nick. He stands at the back of the crowd, his eyes fixed on the speaker.

Of course he's here. No staff is allowed, but Nick is.

I walk up to him and offer a cocktail.

He shakes his head. "I'm good. I don't drink."

Admirable. I rarely drink either. I've seen enough embarrassing behaviors of customers at work, the usual gradual spiral out of control after a number of drinks. It sort of turns you off from hard drinking.

"Non-alcoholic," I say, motioning to the tray in my hand.

"I'm good," he quips, barely looking at me, his eyes boring into the men in the front row.

I hate when people drool over celebrities or rich people

they don't know and are only fascinated with because they are filthy rich. I shift to stand next to Nick, studying the crowd. "Rosenberg doesn't mind that you hang out with the guests?"

Nick snaps his head toward me, his gaze confused. "What do you mean?"

"I mean, staff aren't allowed to mingle, right?"

I can tell I hurt his ego a little.

He shrugs. "I'm not just a driver," he says, slightly hostile. "I'm his assistant. I'm his butler. His right-hand man. He'd fall apart without me."

I bet you shine. That's a lot of credit to take. "The guy is a millionaire, and you work for him."

"The richest people are not necessarily the smartest. I make sure that guy stays in check. If it weren't for me, he'd be broke, or in jail, or dead."

"Whoa. That's ambitious."

Rosenberg's loud laughter at the front jerks Nick's head in his direction.

Rosenberg is exchanging pleasantries with the woman in the white suit. I look between him and Nick and can't figure out if Nick is envious or too dedicated to his boss. He looks like a pet that is upset because he doesn't get enough attention from his master.

"He's a genius," I repeat the words I read in an article. "Mr. Rosenberg," I clarify.

"He's a closet alcoholic and a womanizer," Nick says unusually sharply.

"Harsh."

"If it weren't for IxResearch and this"—he motions to the mansion—"you'd never give him a second look. Am I wrong?"

He turns to me, his gaze burning.

Is he upset? Angry? Envious? I don't blame him. It's disheartening to put everything you have into serving others, whether an employer or a business, and not get any credit for it. I feel like he needs approval.

"Well," I say, intentionally batting my eyelashes at him. "That's why I saved *your* life."

Nick's expression softens, and he bursts into a hushed chuckle.

I smile back. I bet he tries hard to make it in this big world, just like me, whatever the cost. Except, knowing that Rosenberg might be a dangerous man, I'm starting to wonder what the cost is for Nick.

I scan the terrace and catch sight of Julien. He stands in the shadows, out of sight, and he's staring at me.

"Dammit," I mutter. "Julien is watching me like a hawk."

Nick snorts. "Staff patrol is on. You should get back to work," he says, his attention back on the front of the crowd.

I wish I could hang out with Nick—not in my staff uniform, but as a guest. I've served plenty celebrities, but I've never hung out with any, except for off-Broadway stars in the small theaters Cara used to work back in the day.

I start walking among the guests, deliberately making my way toward Julien. His eyes track my movements. I step up to him and offer a drink.

His gaze hardens. "You are not paid to fraternize with the staff," he says coldly.

I fake a smile. "Understood."

I keep the graceful pose, my arm bent behind my back as I walk away, the fake smile plastered on my face as I offer drinks to the guests.

I return to the kitchen for another tray. Rosalie is preoccupied with opening bottles of juice. Meanwhile, I study the bottles of booze lined up on the counter. Whiskey—bingo! I take one of the tall glasses we use for sodas and iced tea and fill it with ice, then fill it to the brim with whiskey. I push a lemon slice onto the rim and stick a straw in. I place the glass on the tray with the other tall glasses, close to me, so that no one takes it, and make my way back to the terrace.

This time, I have a clear destination—Rosenberg.

At your service, sir, I say to myself, and this time, my smile is genuine.

29

ANONYMOUS

Out of the many camera feeds from The Splendors Mansion, only one is of interest to me right now.

I lean closer, watching you approach the entrance.

"Here you are," I whisper, my eyes glued to the screen.

I watch your expression. You are focused. Always are. You didn't know what you were getting yourself into when you came to The Splendors. Lying is hard work, but you are good at it.

"Yes, you are," I whisper bitterly.

You receive a message on your phone, but you're too engrossed in the guests to check it. It's all right. I'll do it for you, as always—every call, every message on your phone is reflected on my spyware app that's synced with your device.

I'm watching you every minute I can. Indoors. Outdoors. At your place, yes, your place. I've been there. It's a shithole. Years of work, and you still don't have anything to show for it, though you think this time will be different.

You seem slightly upset, which is understandable in your position. I'd feel bad for you if I didn't know you better and everything you've done in the past. Including the secret you buried in that cabin in the woods.

You think you have everyone fooled.

Maybe. Just not me. You are an opportunist. I know why you are here. Soon, I'll make all your secrets rain on you all at once.

That's a promise, Nick.

30

NATALIE

The official presentation is over. The crowd disperses across the terrace and the lawn. Many hang out at the Wi-Fi-powered tablet stands. No doubt, these guys are checking the stock markets, making thousands of dollars a minute, even when they are drinking their fancy cocktails.

Rosenberg is chatting to a young girl in a golden mini-dress and sparkly stilettos. Her blond hair is swept to one side and over her shoulder, barely covering her deep cleavage. Her body practically vibrates with pheromones—boobs out, hip cocked. I'm sure she's not a crypto mastermind—she's a huntress. The troubling thing is that she doesn't look old enough to drink. If she were at my bar, I would've carded her without a second thought and watched her drink to make sure no one spiked her.

Rosenberg's hands are in his pants pockets, his white button-up undone at the neck. He's smiling, his gaze now and then sliding to the girl's cleavage, which seems to inch closer and closer to him as the two of them talk.

I can tell he wants to hook up. That whiskey he chugged in the library is already in his system, and more is coming. Let's see what the Crypto King is like when he's hammered.

I approach him with a professional smile. "Drinks?"

I don't look at the blondie, only at Rosenberg. Slowly, I take his special drink off the tray and hand it to him. "Your iced tea, sir," I say, catching a glint of surprise in his eyes.

"Thank you," he says, accepting it.

I look at him like I just met the love of my life, and he gazes back.

"Everything okay?" the blondie chirps, but he doesn't look at her, and I don't break our eye contact. I muster a shy smile, make it disappear, then smile again, projecting timidness, cocking my head at him, faking awe.

"*Ex-cuse me*," the blondie says louder, irritated. "Are you done here?"

I nod and lower my gaze, as if in submission, then step away. Out of the corner of my eye I see Rosenberg take the first sip, and he grunts—freaking *grunts*—in satisfaction.

Mission accomplished. I just need to get him alone, possibly drunk, possibly somewhat incapacitated. That's the only way I can find out if he has any secrets on his phone or on his computer. I can also see what he tries with me, so I can find out what he tried with Cara. I'm his confidante now, after all.

This would've been a good time to pass on any information that the stalker guy wanted me to get to Rosenberg. With so many people around, I could've easily slipped a note into his pocket. Hopefully, another opportunity will come up.

Chin up, I continue my rounds around the back terrace and run right into Julien's cold stare across the terrace. He stands in the shadows, like a security guard, his eyes tracking my movements. I have a feeling he knows that I just served Rosenberg a drink. But no one will question me. No one will assume that I volunteered to break the house rule.

I purposefully stay within earshot of Rosenberg and his huntress, offering drinks to others but paying close attention to what the boss is doing.

That's when Rosenberg leans over to the blondie and says not so inconspicuously, "How about we take this somewhere private? Go check out the library. I'll meet you there in a bit."

Well, that was quick. Rosenberg's on the move.

My pulse spikes—it's time to find out what the Man of the Year is all about.

31

NATALIE

This is the oddest party I've been to.

It's in full swing. The young entrepreneurs drink more than anyone, but I've never served so many energy drinks, healthy juices, and non-alcoholic sparkling concoctions.

"They didn't come here to party," Rosalie explains when I bring it up. "They are networking."

"Yeah, okay. That blondie who was talking to Rosenberg was definitely not networking. Unless spreading her legs 'somewhere private' as per our boss is considered networking."

Rosalie's expression changes. "Keep doing what you are doing, Natalie." She shoves another tray of drinks into my hands and tries to usher me out.

"Should I go check on that girl? She's in the library."

"Natalie?" Rosalie warns me.

"Rosalie?" I cock my head at her.

She gives me a backward nod. "Go do your job. What the boss does in private is none of your business."

Shoving my irritation down, I walk out and turn the

other way, toward the library, when her sharp voice stops me. "Natalie!"

I turn to see Rosalie in the doorway, glaring at me. She jerks her head in the opposite direction.

Ugh.

I turn on my heel and hurry out onto the terrace.

And here's a sight to behold!

Rosenberg stands with his arms spread like a king, a large crowd gathered around him.

"To I! X! Research!" he roars, literally roars, face lifted to the sky as the crowd around him cheers enthusiastically.

"To the power of the digital world!" he roars again, the applause and whistling escalating.

"To the crypto empire!"

The crowd goes wild.

"Cheers!" he roars again, downing the liquid from a champagne flute and pumping the air above him with his fist as the crowd starts chanting, "I! X! I! X! I! X!"

With a drunk grin, Rosenberg stumbles toward the terrace doors.

He's wasted. *Shocker.* I've seen this before, the rapid slide into unruly drunkenness, and that's what Rosenberg is. Either he can't hold his liquor, or it kicks in a bipolar effect on his personality. I get why there's a no-drinking rule at the house, because as Rosenberg walks by me, there's a dangerous burn in his glassy eyes.

My concern is for the blondie in the library.

I hustle between the guests, trying to get rid of the drinks on my tray and collect the empty ones. My nerves are on edge, the blondie on my mind.

It takes me an annoyingly long time, and by the time I walk back into the mansion, something has changed inside.

The house is empty of guests. A tall figure blocks the hallway that goes from the living room toward the east wing—it's Dave, the security guard.

My stomach turns with unease.

I notice another figure behind him, by the door to the library. It's Nick. He stands motionless. His head is lowered, eyes on the floor—he's eavesdropping!

Oh, wow. This house works like a well-oiled machine. I wonder if the entire staff is committed to saving Rosenberg's reputation. Or...

An awful thought makes my blood go cold—what if I set up Rosenberg for another crime? What if something horrible is about to happen to the blondie?

I don't want her to get in trouble. Maybe she'll have a good time. Maybe she'll become Rosenberg's new secretary or wife. Wouldn't that be a jackpot for her?

The word "jackpot" makes me think of Cara. She thought Rosenberg would be just that.

Crap, crap, crap, my mind spins on repeat.

I step into the doorway that leads to the staff kitchen and peek from behind it down the hallway, narrowing my eyes on Nick in the distance, who opens the door to the library and walks in, shutting the door behind him.

I have to know what's happening, so I step out and march down the hall, across the living room, and walk up to Dave, who immediately blocks my way.

"Aren't you supposed to be at the gate?" I ask him politely.

"Not right now. Keep doing what you are doing." He motions for me to go away.

"Is everything okay?" I insist, glancing between him and the library door.

He takes a threatening step toward me. "I said, move it."

I hear loud voices and arguing coming from the library, then Rosenberg's shout, "Piss oooooff, you asshole!"

"What's happening?" I repeat.

Dave ducks his head at me, glaring. "Mind your own business. Get back to work."

Suddenly, he raises his hand to his earpiece and cocks his head, then presses the push-to-talk button on his lapel.

"Understood," he says, then walks over to the wall and kills the lights in the hallway.

"I said, go," he mouths to me.

That very moment, Nick's head pops out of the library. "Julien! I need Julien! Right now!" he shouts.

Dave presses the push-to-talk button again. "Julien. Library. Urgent. It's Rosenberg."

That's when I hear a female scream from the library, followed by something breaking. It's the next sound that makes my heart still—a gunshot.

32

ANONYMOUS

Look at that, you screwed up again. Oops! How typical of you.

I watch you brandish the gun on camera. You just shot at the ceiling. That's happened before. Any other time, I would've laughed, but my eyes caught sight of the girl in the armchair.

She's motionless.

I rewind the footage and watch how everything unfolds. It's the first time I see it bright and clear, happening right on camera. Again…

This has to be fixed. Right now.

I grind my teeth.

You are a liar. Your past is full of shameful secrets. Everything is spiraling out of control. That's what lies do—they infect, fester, and then come to the surface.

When I'm done with you, you'll be just one more checkmark for me and another case for the police.

You wanted to shine, Mr. Rosenberg? Well, I'll make you burn.

33

NATALIE

Julien runs past Dave and me like a rocket and disappears into the library.

More shouting follows from there, then the sound of smashed glass. I hear fast-approaching footsteps, and another security guard, Steve, comes running and disappears into the library too.

Oh my god, this is an emergency! Something is going down, and there's nothing I can do. I crane my neck toward the library, but Dave steps sideways to block the view.

"Go. Away," he hisses.

I turn on my heel and run to the kitchen where Rosalie is pouring purple drinks into champagne flutes.

"Rosalie!" I shout. "Something's happening in the library."

Without stopping what she is doing, she looks at me from under her brows. "What's happening?"

"Both security guys are there. Julien. Nick. There was a gunshot, I swear," I blurt as fast as I can. "Someone is fighting in the library. Rosenberg is there."

She doesn't even flinch at my words. "Natalie, mind your own business," she says calmly. "Here." She passes me a new tray of drinks. "Terrace. Now. You have a job to do."

Argh! I'm practically steaming with fury.

"Really?" I snap at her. "I just told you that Rosenberg is with a young girl, there was a gunshot, and—"

"Now!" she barks, glaring at me. "You want to get paid, don't you?"

"Fine!" I grab the tray and stomp out of the kitchen and into the hallway, but then I stop and turn in the direction of the library.

Low moans come from behind the library door. They are barely audible, and one would've missed them if they weren't listening. But there's no one around but me and Dave farther down the hallway, like a statue, his stare trained on me from the distance.

"You imbeciles!" comes Rosenberg's roar from behind the library door. "You don't know what's going on!"

There is the sound of a struggle, but that's not what petrifies me. With all those voices, there's not a peep from the girl.

I'm panting, thinking about what to do.

Suddenly, the library door swings open, and three figures stumble out. I step back to hide behind the corner and peek out.

It's dark, but I can see Steve, who has Rosenberg in a headlock. My eyes widen as Rosenberg is led, like he's arrested, toward the living room and up the main stairs. Nick hurries after them. Rosenberg is hissing out curses and making angry animal sounds. Dave, the other security guy, observes them calmly, like it's nothing out of the ordinary.

Again, Rosenberg is not my concern right now. The girl is. What did he do to her? Why isn't she running out of the library? And if I haven't missed anything, Julien is still in the library with her.

Dave presses his finger to his earpiece, listening, then speaks into the mic, "Unconscious? Drunk? Yes, I'll get a car."

The words make my head spin.

The girl can't be unconscious. I observed her on the terrace. She barely drank. She was more or less sober when she walked to the library. It's been less than an hour. She can't be drunk!

That's when I know—this is serious. As serious as Cara, and Darla, and probably many before them.

If I'm not mistaken, this is a cover-up.

Blood pounding between my ears, I make a split-second decision.

34

NATALIE

This will cost me a job and money and might put me in danger, but I can't watch another person being poisoned.

I dart to the locker, set down the tray with drinks, and retrieve my phone. I have to get help for the girl.

Hands trembling, I dial Detective Dupin's number.

She picks up right away. "Detective Dupin."

"Hello? Detective? It's Natalie Olsen from the hospital. It's about my friend Cara, the unconscious girl from the bus stop," I blurt as fast as I can and, phone pressed to my ear, dash toward the library.

"Yes, Miss Olsen. How can I help you?" Detective Dupin rasps.

Dave is still in the hallway, talking to someone through the earpiece. He makes a move to stop me, but I raise my phone in front of me.

"Emergency! Step aside!" I blurt, registering his wide-eyed confusion. While he hesitates for a second, I slip past him, dart into the library, lock the door, and press my back to it.

"Miss Olsen?" the detective repeats.

The first thing I see is the blondie's motionless body splayed in the armchair, her limp arms hanging down the sides, chin resting on her chest.

Julien, down on one knee, has his fingers on her neck, checking her pulse. Right away, his startled eyes dart to me, then shift to my phone.

"I'm at Geoffrey Rosenberg's house," I blurt into the phone as Julien shoots up to his feet. "I'm here because—"

Julien crosses the distance between us in several quick strides and knocks the phone out of my hand. In a split second, his arm is around me, restraining me from behind, his other hand tightly covering my mouth.

I try to thrash and scream, but all that comes out of my mouth is a low, inarticulate sound as Julien's arm holds me tightly against his hard body.

"Be. Quiet," he whispers in a voice laced with danger.

"Miss Olsen?" I hear the voice on the phone that lies on the floor several feet away.

"Don't fight," Julien whispers, his lips brushing against my ear. "Don't scream," he warns. "What you do next is *very* important. Understood?"

My heart is raging against my ribs. Blood pounds in my head.

"Shhh," Julien calms me. He's not hurting me, but his hold is steel-hard, making it impossible to move.

"Tell me that you understand," he repeats.

A nod is all I can manage. He can kill me, kill me right now. Or poison me. Or whatever he does here with women.

"Who did you call?" Julien asks. "I'm going to let my hand go, and you won't scream, okay? It's very important that you stay quiet, Natalie. You scream, and things are going to turn bad. I need to know who you're talking to."

Slowly, he lets go of my mouth.

"Detective Dupin," I answer, my voice breaking.

My mind is silently screaming. This might be the end of me, but at least if I disappear or end up in the hospital, the detective will be able to trace my phone call to this house.

"I'm talking to Detective Dupin," I say, panting, my body shaking against Julien's, who's still holding me against him. "If I don't answer, she will track the signal and send the police here."

Abruptly, Julien's arm loosens around me, and he steps in front of me, his eyes burning with an intensity I've never seen before. I don't know what he's thinking, but the way he looks at me is the extreme opposite of friendly.

"I need you to pick up your phone," he says calmly, "and tell the detective that you will call them back, understood?"

"I just told her where I am," I quip. "You can't harm me. It's too late, Julien."

He doesn't even flinch. Instead, he slowly picks up the phone off the floor and passes it to me.

"Answer," he says barely audibly. "Say you will call back. Nothing funny, Natalie. Or you won't walk out of here tonight."

"They will find you," I snarl at him.

"Not before they find *you*," he says, anger flashing in his eyes.

I swallow hard and do as I'm told. "Detective? Sorry," I blurt into the phone. "I'm at work and just had a question but dropped my phone."

"Is everything all right?" Detective Dupin asks in a concerned voice.

Julien's eyes drill into me. He's towering above me. He's intimidating. He's waiting. And he can't do anything about me now, because the person on the phone—a detective, no less—knows where I am.

Blood is pounding between my ears, my chest rising in heavy breathing, and I want to cry, but in relief. I outsmarted them. I have backup. No matter what happens now, Rosenberg's house is already on the detective's radar.

"Miss Olsen?" Detective Dupin insists. "What's going on? Where are you?"

Julien blinks slowly and tips his chin at the phone. "Answer," he mouths.

"Hi. Sorry again. I… Um…" I try to bring my thoughts in order, my entire body trembling, along with my voice. "I got a job. At *Geoffrey Rosenberg*'s mansion," I repeat, accentuating the name. There. I tip my chin at Julien in victory. "I wanted to talk to you about Cara's case. I have some information for you. Can I call you later though?"

"Sure," the detective says.

"This is my number."

I would've smiled in triumph at Julien if I weren't petrified right now—of Rosenberg, of what happened to the girl, and of what happens next.

I pant so hard that my throat and chest hurt. Julien is frozen in his spot, his unblinking stare on me.

I have to be smart about this. So I add, "Detective, if I don't call you within a couple of hours, will you call me back? Please?"

The last words make me want to punch the air. I think I might've just avoided something horrible.

35

ANONYMOUS

I lean back in my computer chair and stare at the live camera feed of the library on my monitor.

The two of you stand chest to chest like lovers or enemies—I can't figure it out, but it's amusing.

You are a Good Samaritan, Natalie. I gave you too little credit. You did the right thing, and you think you are safe.

But you just made things a whole lot worse.

I can hear your heavy breathing on the other end as I hold the phone to my ear.

"Yes, I will do that, Miss Olsen. Stay safe," I say into the phone and hang up.

36

NATALIE

This place is going down, I promise myself. I grind my teeth as I hang up the phone and triumphantly stare back at Julien.

I tilt my head toward the motionless girl. "She isn't drunk, just so you know. She was poisoned, sedated, spiked—I don't know what it is, but it's not booze."

Julien's expression doesn't change, but his nostrils flare just a little bit. He might be good at self-control, but he's not calm.

"What makes you think that?" he asks.

I take a tiny step toward him, the poky end of my neckerchief almost touching his suit. Rising on my toes, I bring my face closer to his.

"Because I watched her walk in here an hour ago," I hiss. "She was *fine*. She wasn't even tipsy. That"—I nod toward the motionless body—"is not from booze. She needs help, Julien. She needs to be taken to the hospital. And if you don't let me take her, the detective I just talked to will know what happened. In fact, she will learn about the previous house-keeper and much more."

Julien's eyes narrow slightly, like he's trying to figure out whether I'm making this up. He can probably tell that I'm trembling, nervous, despite my angry voice. I don't care.

He presses the mic button on his lapel. "Dave, I need you here."

He steps to the library door to unlock it and lets the security guy in.

Of course, Dave glares at me. He should get a prize for the angriest eyes, though I'm pretty sure I'm the only person he directs his glares at.

Julien motions for him with two fingers to follow and walks up to the blondie. "This young lady needs to get to the hospital ASAP." He picks up her purse, weeds out the driver's license, and snaps a picture of it.

Meanwhile, Dave picks up the girl in his arms like she weighs nothing and, giving me a side-eye, walks out.

Julien follows. "Clean this up," he tells me with a nod to the shattered glass on the floor.

I dart after him into the dark hallway and call out, "Julien?"

He stops, turning to look at me.

"If she doesn't get to the hospital," I say, "she might not make it. And if she doesn't, I'll find out. And…" He knows what *and* means. "Please, help her," I say and walk back into the library.

I let out a shaky breath as I close the door behind me. The library suddenly seems too quiet and eerie, the glass shards on the floor glistening in the lamplight.

I should get my purse and run the hell away from here while there are witnesses and bodyguards all over the parking lot. Instead, something stops me.

I take deep breaths, calming myself, listening to the

sounds in the house. The noise from the party on the terrace doesn't reach here. Nor do any sounds from upstairs. It's quiet up there, which makes me wonder what Nick and Rosenberg are up to.

The change in Rosenberg was drastic, violent even. It's not common, but I've seen it plenty of times before. Once, a customer at my bar got so angry about being cut off that he took a glass and smashed it against the bar counter with his hand. Blood everywhere, glass shards stuck in his palm, he shoved it in my face, laughing like a lunatic.

That's Rosenberg, though he was interrupted in time. Was he? What does he do to women after he drugs them?

My brain is reeling as I study the mess on the floor, about to bring a broom, when my eyes catch an unusual object under the armchair. It looks like a piece of candy. When I walk over and sit on my haunches to take a closer look, I realize that it's not a candy but a flat, red, rectangular cartridge, about three inches long. I pick it up with my thumb and forefinger and bring it closer to my face, studying it.

One end has a knob, like a button. A small needle protrudes from the other end.

My blood goes cold—it's a syringe.

37

NATALIE

It's almost ten o'clock, an hour since the incident, and my hands are still shaking as I pick up the empty plates and glasses on the back terrace and bring them to the kitchen. Rosalie looks like Grumpy Cat, not a word about what happened in the library.

I feel nervous tremors all over my body. My stress level is higher than it was during my shift on New Year's Eve at a Presidential Club's bar two years ago. Am I being watched? I have no doubt anymore. Just in case, I keep my phone on me. If they want to fire me for it, I don't care.

Most guests left. A few are still chatting, sipping their colorful fizzy drinks. Surprisingly, no one is drunk. A number of people are on their laptops, and someone is doing a full-on computer presentation in one corner of the terrace. While these people are partying, a person got assaulted, and they don't have a clue.

Julien walks out onto the terrace and beckons me with two fingers.

"Where's the girl?" I ask as I approach.

He motions to the door. "Come with me."

"Julien?" I insist, not moving. "Where's the girl?"

"I said, inside," he snaps, making my stomach turn. Julien doesn't snap. He doesn't raise his voice, doesn't lose composure. Except tonight.

We walk down the hallway to the staff kitchen. It's empty. No Rosalie. No catering staff.

"I thought you were supposed to keep an eye on everyone here," I say bitterly and cross my arms over my chest.

A familiar voice out in the hall approaches, and Nick storms into the kitchen, followed by Rosalie.

"He was *not* supposed to drink tonight!" Nick shouts, whipping around to confront her as she lowers her head submissively, her eyes cast down. "How did he get ahold of booze? How?"

It's the first time I've seen him angry. He stalls when he notices me, but his eyes right away shift to Julien. He steps up to him and grits out, "*Ex-plain.*"

Julien's jaw tics. "I saw one of the caterers give him a drink. It looked like iced tea."

I still like an iron rod. Julien just covered for me. Nick is the one who hired me, I'm sure he wouldn't say anything to me. So then why did Julien lie?

"Iced tea?" Nick snarls. "Iced tea doesn't get him deliriously drunk. Why didn't you check?"

"Check what, Nick?" Julien asks, standing in front of him in his usual bodyguard pose. "What was I supposed to do? Come up in front of a hundred people to my boss, take the drink out of his hand, and sniff it?"

Nick ruffles his hair, rolling his neck in annoyance.

"The caterers weren't warned about Mr. Rosenberg and

alcohol," Julien continues, blinking slowly. "We can't exactly tell them, 'Don't serve booze to the guy who owns the house, the billion-dollar company, and everyone else around.' And we can't tell them he has a drinking problem. Not now. Not when his company is about to grow tenfold in value."

Nick rubs his face with both hands, exhaling in frustration. "We are all supposed to make sure things go smoothly. Not like the last time. But here we are!" Nick looks at Julien again. "Did you send the girl home?"

"Yes."

My eyes snap at Julien, who ignores me like I'm not here. *Send her home?* That's how Nick put it? Does he even know she was drugged?

Nick sighs loudly and leans on the counter with both hands, hanging his head. "When he wakes up tomorrow, I'm *so* fired. All of us are."

Rosalie looks from under her eyebrows between Nick and Julien. "If I lose my job, I'm blaming you two."

That makes Nick chuckle as he pushes off the counter and walks toward the door. His last words before he walks out are, "Let's hope he doesn't ruin our lives in revenge."

38

NATALIE

"Your shift is over," Julien says to me when Nick walks out. "Meet me outside when you get your stuff."

I get my things out of the locker and walk out into the night. It's quiet outside. Someone must've turned off the music on the terrace. At the front of the house, car doors slam and tires hiss against the driveway as the last guests leave. There's no one around, and this might not be a good time to be alone with Julien, but I need answers.

"What did you do with the girl?" I ask as I stop in front of him.

We are standing just outside the staff entrance. The night is pleasant, but this place suffocates me with its secrets. I can't wait to get out of here.

"We took her to her place and called 911," Julien says, his hands in his pockets.

"And you know where she lives?"

"We know everything about all our guests. This is not exactly the average Joe's crowd."

"She was unconscious, Julien. I heard a gunshot. Tell me what happened."

He doesn't answer.

"Tell me or I'm going to the police!"

"We don't discuss these episodes," he says. "We just deal with them."

"Oh, you just go along?" I mock him. "You need to report Rosenberg."

"We'll all lose our jobs."

"So what?" I shout.

He looks around, then steps closer. "No one needs to hear that," he says in a hushed voice.

"Oh, yeah? So he can keep drugging women and do god knows what with them while he's drunk?"

"That's why we keep him at bay. And we can't go to the police. He's about to make IxResearch public. Thousands of people's well-being depends on that."

"Screw the company! Screw *you*, Julien! I used to bartend. I saw this sort of thing all the time. I know how it goes. I know guys like you who sweep shit like this under the carpet."

"Natalie—"

"You watch others do this sort of stuff and you are, like, none of my business? Yeah? Bravo, Julien."

"Nata—"

"Someone's life gets ruined, and you don't care. Except when it hits too close to home."

"Natalie, you are wrong and—"

"Darla was an employee. Despite her unprofessional behavior, she didn't deserve what she got."

I shut up and watch his expression change.

Yeah, I struck a nerve. It makes me wonder why he covers

for Rosenberg, why everyone in this house does. What does Rosenberg have on everyone that they all dance to his tune?

"I need to know that the blond girl is fine," I demand.

Or I swear, I'll make sure everyone in this house goes to jail. But I don't tell Julien that. I need to get home safe first and talk to the detective.

"The girl is fine," he says.

"And you know that how?"

"I just received a report that she is logged into the hospital system. She's stable."

Somehow, I believe him, my anger dissipating in seconds. But I'll ask the detective to confirm that.

"Please, don't discuss this with anyone, Natalie. It's in your best interest."

Oh, look who's being nice now. "Is it? Are you threatening me?"

I'm sure he's alluding to my conversation with the detective, but you bet I'm going to have a talk with her.

Nothing changes in his face. "I'm asking you. You shouldn't be in this house, not around Rosenberg, not involved in this whole business."

Why is he so afraid that I'm around, afraid that this gets out? He doesn't show it, but he's wary. His tone has changed.

The silence between us is razor sharp, and when he reaches inside his suit, I flinch. A split-second thought crosses my mind that he can overpower me in seconds, make me vanish, or I'll end up unconscious at a bus stop tomorrow morning. One injection—

"Here." He pulls out what looks like an envelope.

I let out a relieved breath. "What is this?"

"Your pay."

"That's for three days?"

"Yes. And for you to not show up tomorrow."

"Why? Is that you suddenly being a concerned citizen?"

"That's me protecting you."

"I don't need your protection, Julien."

"Or so you think."

"I'm not a quitter."

He rubs the top of his head with his palm, the movement casual but out of character. Tonight, everyone is on edge, including Mister-I'm-In-Control-House-Manager.

Julien's eyes are on me again. Silence burns between us as I'm trying to figure out if we are on the same team, same wave, or same hate train. I really am starting to hate everyone in this mansion.

"I didn't mean to be rough," Julien says apologetically, which confuses me more than him trying to fire me. "Back in the library—I apologize for mishandling you."

His apology takes me aback. His sudden change in the way he treats me even more so. Julien's gaze on me is so intense that I'm starting to worry about the meaning behind it.

That moment when you see want in a guy's eyes—it's powerful. You learn to detect it when you work with people.

Nick wants me, but he's too ambitious and too close to the boss to be really interested in a cleaning lady.

Rosenberg doesn't want me, but he's interested for other reasons. There's something dark about his dealings with women.

Julien is different. I can't figure him out. I often catch him staring at me. At first, I thought he was protective of his workspace. Then, I figured it was curiosity. There are moments when I think he's interested in me. He might be the type who needs time to get to know people. Or...

If it's *or*, he could be a Pandora's box. I've met those before. Some of the quietest people in bars have the loudest stories to tell. There are those whose stories never reach the light. There are psychopaths. They are master manipulators. Some play nice, side with the law, though in fact, they are the executioners, willing to cover up about anything and "deal" with emergency situations in their own screwed-up way.

Julien might be playing more games in this house than anyone. In that case, I should be careful, because that means he's a controlling kind, the quiet one. And *that's* the most dangerous type.

39

NATALIE

As soon as Julien goes back inside, I walk to my car, get in, and lean back against the driver's seat, closing my eyes in relief.

All the staff was on edge earlier. It's as if everyone has been trying to prevent something horrible from happening. Something Rosenberg has done before. I can't wrap my head around it, and no one is telling me anything.

I have chill pills in the glove compartment. I need a dozen to calm my nerves, but I won't take them—I need to stay clearheaded. Inside my car feels like home, it feels somewhat *safe*, and as seconds go by, the noisy thoughts in my head fade.

Loud rapping against the driver's window makes me jump.

"Jesus," I mutter. It's Nick. I roll down the window. "Hey, stranger."

"Sorry about tonight," he says, though I'm not sure why he is the one apologizing.

I shrug.

"What a clusterfuck, eh?" He blurts out a short laugh.

"What happened tonight? With Mr. Rosenberg and that girl?" I ask.

If Julien doesn't tell me, maybe Nick will. I'm being careful. It looks like everyone has their own version of the story.

"Hell if I know," Nick murmurs and rubs the back of his neck. "Rosenberg got drunk. I don't know how. That's why we have the rule that *he* enforced. He has issues. And he can't afford to make an ass out of himself. Not right now."

"Why?"

"IxResearch announced its IPO and is going public on Monday. It's important. Billions of dollars in investments are at stake."

"Why is everyone more concerned about money and not the fact that he could have hurt that blond he was talking to?"

Nick cocks his head to the side. "Hurt?"

Crap, I shouldn't have said anything. "I mean, I heard him shouting. I cleaned the library afterward. There was all that broken glass. So much of it. *He* did that?"

"Yeah. We call them *episodes*."

"That's one hell of a temper."

Nick looks away. That's the first time he doesn't joke around.

"I mean, the girl was drunk," he says hesitantly.

"Drunk? I saw her an hour before that. She seemed fine."

"Well, she wasn't."

"Does this happen—"

"Natalie, listen." Nick shuts his eyes and pinches the bridge of his nose. He stands still for a moment. When he looks at me again, his gaze is almost pleading. "Please, don't tell anyone about it. Not a word," he says almost in a whisper.

"Not until Monday. Otherwise, we will lose our jobs, and everything will turn into a giant mess."

Right, here's another person trying to cover up what happened.

"Please?" He gives me puppy eyes. "I need this job. And I don't want... Ugh. The boss can be pretty cruel when it comes to..." He doesn't finish the sentence and looks away.

"What do you mean by cruel?"

"He's a powerful man, okay? He can ruin someone's life just like that." He snaps his fingers and lets out another heavy sigh. "Anyway. I don't want to talk about it. I don't want to talk about tonight. Or the party. Or freaking Rosenberg." He yanks a set of keys out of his pocket and starts swinging them back and forth. It seems to be his relaxation technique. He finally meets my eyes. "Wanna get out of here?" he asks, seemingly calmer. "Go for a drink?"

That's one hell of a topic change.

"You don't drink," I remind him.

He chuckles. "You look like you could use one."

Before I have a chance to say anything else, he leans with his hands on the driver's door, ducking his head so he can look at me. "Let's get out of here, forget about this hot mess of a party. Let's chat or whatever," he offers softly, his hopeful eyes on me. Then his hand reaches inside the car and tucks a loose strand of my hair behind my ear.

My breath hitches in my throat, and I don't know how to respond to this gesture.

"Chat, huh?" I could chat. I could get *him* to chat for sure. A drink sounds good. I need a bottle to relax. I'm exhausted. I really need to clear my head, and Nick sounds perfect.

The staff door suddenly swings open, and Rosalie appears. She takes several steps toward the parking lot, her hands set on her hips, as if she's a mom who has just seen her adolescent daughter flirt with an older boy.

"Nick?" she calls out, which is annoying and sounds like "Neeeeeek."

Nick doesn't look away from me, as if he doesn't give a crap.

"Nee-eeeck?" she calls out again.

Nick rolls his eyes and pushes off the car, turning toward her. "Yes, Rosalie!" he says, punctuating each word with annoyance.

"Boss just tried to come downstairs. We need you," she says.

He turns toward me and just gazes at me for a while. There's sadness in his eyes. He looks tired. I don't think he wants to go back in.

"I have to go," he whispers.

It sounds almost like a plea, like he needs saving. My shift is over, and I wish I could take him with me. But The Splendors' staff... Well, they're in this too deep.

"See you tomorrow, doll," Nick says.

He walks past Rosalie and disappears inside the house, while Rosalie stands with her hands still on her hips, her eyes fixed on me. She's waiting for me to leave.

Whatever.

I pull out of the parking lot, and even before I leave the premises, I dial Detective Dupin.

This shady enterprise, called The Splendors, is going down.

40

ANONYMOUS

I really, really like you, Natalie. If we met in a different place and at a different time, we could've been friends.

But fate is a wild card. This will be over soon.

I see your number flash on my phone and pick up. "Detective Dupin."

41

NATALIE

"Detective Dupin," the low raspy voice says.

"Detective? Hi," I say into the phone. "This is Natalie Olsen again."

"Miss Olsen, how are you?"

I feel more confident being on the phone with a detective as I drive through The Splendors' gate on my way out.

"I wanted to tell you that I know the man my friend went home with after the club."

"Do you?"

"Yes. Geoffrey Rosenberg. Does it ring a bell?"

"Should it?"

Just then, I pass a car parked on the side of the street. When I look in the rearview mirror, its headlights come on, and it pulls onto the road just a short distance behind me.

Crap. Is someone following me again?

"Miss Olsen?" the detective calls out to me.

"Yes, sorry."

"You were saying?"

"Geoffrey Rosenberg is an entrepreneur, a very wealthy one. Google him. I recognized him when I ran into him by accident," I lie. If I tell her I saw him on a magazine cover, she might think I'm after his money. "And I got a job as a cleaning lady at his house."

"You did what?"

Ugh. That sounded bad.

"I had to make sure," I say, trying not to sound careless or worse—like a gold digger. "You said there was another person in the hospital who was brought in with the same condition as my friend. Is her name Darla?"

"Miss Olsen, sounds like you are doing some type of amateur investigation, and, to be honest, it's slightly unsettling."

"Detective, I'm sure the man my friend went home with is Geoffrey Rosenberg. A hundred percent. In fact, there's a young woman who was at a party at his house tonight who ended up at a hospital. She is…" I realize I didn't even ask Julien her name or what hospital she was taken to.

"What's her name?"

"I don't know."

"Uh-huh."

I slam the steering wheel in frustration. The detective doesn't sound like she believes me. I look in the rearview mirror—the car is still following me. When I take a ramp onto the highway, it does the same.

"And you went to that party, too?" the detective asks.

"No! Gah! I *work* at that house. I have for three days now."

"And how exactly did you get a job at that place?"

"By coincidence." If I tell her that I coincidentally saved his driver's life in Manhattan, she'll definitely think I'm either lying or a loon.

"A coincidence," the detective repeats.

"Yes. I know how it sounds—"

"Is there something you are not telling me, Miss Olsen?"

Here it goes again. She talks to me like I'm trying to mislead her.

"Everything I've told you is true," I say. "If you check the local hospitals, I'm sure you will find a young woman admitted several hours ago, spiked by a heavy drug." If Julien lied, and she wasn't taken to the hospital, I'm really screwed. The detective won't ever trust me again.

"Anything else you want to tell me? Anything regarding your friend?" she asks.

"No. But something's not right about the mansion I work at. Or Geoffrey Rosenberg. I think there are a lot more victims than just Cara and the girl tonight. It's serious."

"Miss Olsen, here's what I suggest. You don't go back to that house. You don't do anything that might put you in danger. You don't talk to anyone about it. You stay put. Right now, everything you say sounds like slander."

My jaw drops. "Excuse me?"

"Without any proof, what you are saying is a serious accusation. Considering you say the man is wealthy, this might turn against you very fast, in a way that could put you on the wrong side of the law."

"What do you mean? My friend is a victim, and I'm trying to help!"

"Miss Olsen? There's no need to yell at me. All I'm saying is that I want you to stay safe. Keep everything you told me to yourself. No discussing this with anyone, so you don't tarnish a man's reputation before we have any sort of evidence. You don't want to be accused of stalking."

"I'm a witness! What other evidence do you need?"

"Miss Olsen, you said he is a wealthy man. He probably has

many important connections and a big business. Many people try to profit off others' success, if you know what I mean."

Suddenly, the detective's words sink in. Oh, and they sink in like a thousand-pound barrel.

Rich man. Connections. Business. Poor woman's accusations. No evidence. Slander.

The words spin in a circle in my head, and I see it clearly just as I saw it the day I found out who Rosenberg was—a poor person, and a woman at that, has no power to bring a wealthy man down.

I grit my teeth, waiting for Detective Dupin to talk.

"Let's do one thing," she says in a businesslike voice. "For now, stay away from that man. I will check the hospitals, get some info about this Rosenberg fella, and get in touch with you. Sound good?"

I nod, though she can't see me.

"Miss Olsen. I need to hear it from you. I want you to promise me that you won't play a detective and put yourself in danger."

She doesn't even know the man, but she's warning me. Danger, danger, danger—that's all I hear around Rosenberg, and it's making me sick to my stomach.

"Understood," I say disappointedly. "Can I ask you for a favor?"

"Sure."

"If I don't call you in several days, will you come looking for me? And if you can't find me, will you take this investigation seriously?"

"Miss Olsen—"

"Thank you," I say before she answers and hang up.

I slap the steering wheel in irritation. Anger boils in my veins. No one is willing to investigate Rosenberg.

I look in the rearview mirror and see the headlights behind me. Except now, I'm off the highway and driving through downtown Jersey City, and I can't quite tell if it's the same car following me or not.

The traffic light ahead turns yellow. I speed up and run the red light. That's definitely a ticket, dammit, but at least I think I lost the car behind me.

As I get to my neighborhood, I make an intricate pattern driving around several blocks, just in case I still have the tail, until I finally reach my apartment building and park. I scan the dark street and get out of the car.

I've worked at The Splendors Mansion for only three days, and already I feel unsafe. I feverishly punch in the entrance code to my building and burst inside the foyer just as a person rushes past me, shouldering me. The person is so quick that when I whip around, I only catch the hunching figure, hands in the pockets, hoodie up—no way to see the face or hair color. I stick my head outside, watching the figure hurry away with a slight limp, disappearing into the night.

Odd.

I walk to my apartment and jump, startled, when the fire exit door slams shut at the end of the hallway.

Christ! I'm going to become a nervous wreck if I keep this job.

Inside my apartment, I slump against the hallway wall, relieved, taking deep breaths. One more day down.

A large manila envelope on the floor catches my attention, instantly making my skin crawl—another message. Inside my place. Again!

A scratching noise distracts me.

Ugh, Trixy is probably starving. Except I stall, hearing a little rat-squeal—it's coming from the kitchen.

Can't be…

I step into the kitchen doorway and see Trixy next to an overturned box of Froot Loops cereal, the colorful rings sprinkled all over the counter, Trixy still like an opossum.

"Seriously?"

Trixy doesn't protest when I pick her up and carry her to the cage. The little pest might be in a glucose coma after the Froot Loops feast. Serves her right. How in the world did she get out—

I stop short when I see the cage. It's not the open door with the broken lock that startles me. It's the treasure box that keeps it closed and never moves.

The sight makes the hairs at the back of my neck stand on end. The treasure box is not near the cage—it's on the bureau next to it. And I wish rats could talk so that Trixy could tell me who the hell has been inside my apartment, moving things around.

42

NATALIE

I'm exhausted, but more than that, I'm mad.

I put Trixy back in the cage, turn, and study everything in my apartment with scrupulous attention. This place is a mess, and I can't tell if someone has searched it, but I have no doubt about it. My treasure box didn't just grow legs or wings and transport itself onto the bureau. It hasn't been moved in months, ever since the cage door lock broke.

Then I catch sight of the envelope on the floor. Whoever left it might be the same person who let themselves in. The person who walked past me? Someone who used the fire exit door?

I rip the envelope open. Inside is a note and a smaller envelope, signed, *"For Rosenberg."*

The note is a stained piece of printer paper.

Wait for my call. DO NOT open the small envelope—it's NOT for you.

I swear, I'll kill that guy!

My phone rings. Unknown number. I pick up.

"How dare you break into my place, you asshole?" I snap. "I'm going to call the police—"

"Chill out! Christ! It wasn't me! Calm down!"

"Yeah, okay. And the envelope wasn't you either?"

"It was. I slipped it in under the door. Someone was in your apartment earlier, though."

"How would you know? If that was you—"

"I said, relax! I came to leave a message, and someone was opening your apartment door. I figured a friend of yours, so I waited at the fire stairs. Except the weather is too warm for a hoodie, so the person looked off. Limping, too."

I swallow hard. "None of my friends have keys to my apartment." I instantly think of the person I ran into on my way into the building.

"They sure had a key." A nasty chuckle follows. "Told you. Watch your back. You are already on a hit list."

"Don't try to—"

"I'm joking! Christ! But you *are* being watched. I just know it."

"Yeah, because you are a stalker." I walk to the window and, just in case, shut the blinds.

"Yeah, good call on the blinds."

"Are you kidding me?" I hiss. He *is* watching me. "I thought you didn't want to call my phone."

"Good girl. So, you remembered. I'm calling from a random convenience store. Your calls might already be tracked. My phone's location is not. Next time you get in touch, do not call me from your phone."

"I didn't say I'd ever get in touch."

"Yeah, okay, we'll see. So, about the envelope. No one,

I repeat, *no one* can see that envelope besides Rosenberg. No one can see you give it to him. In fact, it'd be better for you if he didn't see you with that envelope either."

"Well, that ship has sailed."

"What's that supposed to mean?"

"That I'm quitting."

"No, you're not."

"Oh, yeah? You gonna tell me what to do?" I wish he were here so I could punch him in the nose. I'm done with men who boss me around.

"I need you to go back."

"I bet you do. What's in the envelope?"

"Some info for Rosenberg's eyes only."

"And how am I supposed to give it to him without giving it to him?" I mock.

"Figure out how. If he gets the envelope, I can guarantee a payday for us. If you get caught with that thing, you are in trouble. So, don't get caught."

I don't care about the money. I'm not into extortion, or whatever this is. Clearly, this dude is walking a fine line.

"I want something else in return," I say, mulling over the options.

"What's that?"

"I need whatever dirt you have on Rosenberg."

His response is a loud cackle. "Sweetheart, when I'm done with him, that info won't be any good to you."

"You don't know that. It's not for me anyway."

"Ah-ah. Don't get carried away. You are not smart enough to play with the big fish."

I have a strong urge to poke his eyes out right now. "I need that info. You can keep your money."

"Hmm." I know he's trying to figure out what my angle

here is. "Whatever game you are playing, have at it. But only when I get my pay."

"Deal."

"Call me tomorrow when you get it done."

Just like that, he hangs up.

If there's a way to implicate Rosenberg, if all else fails, this stalker guy probably knows how to do it.

And just like that, I don't think I have an option—I have to go back to The Splendors.

DAY 4

43

NATALIE

"She is getting better," the nurse says as soon as I walk into Cara's hospital room.

Right away, I rush to Cara's bed, trying to figure out what exactly changed, though she looks the same—motionless, peaceful.

"Her brain functions are improving," the nurse explains. "That, by any definition, is a spectacular sign."

I smile broadly. It is. Must be the muffins. Though Cara still hasn't come to.

"Hey, babe," I say as I set the box with muffins and a coffee tray on the side table. "Banana ones today. Also, hazelnut coffee. In case you missed it."

I watched a movie once about someone in a coma, and the doctor said that smells, sounds, and touch can heighten brain activity.

It's Sunday. Most people with regular jobs have the day off. I am with my friend who, only a week ago, was singing in the kitchen, cooking breakfast and making plans for the next week. Now we are here.

I pop the lid off Cara's coffee, letting the smell spread around, overriding the hospital room stuffiness. Then I take a seat in the chair next to her bed and slowly drink mine with a banana muffin.

"Trixy escaped," I tell her as I eat. "For a short while, at least. She managed to overturn a box of cereal. It was probably the most glorious five minutes of her life."

I don't like the taste of the muffin, but I eat it, somehow hoping that this routine will force the universe to set things straight—to what they used to be, with Cara safe and sound. Now that I think about it, I don't even like muffins. It was always Cara and Lindsey's thing.

"Someone broke into our place," I say, updating Cara. "I'm pretty sure any expert search party would fail to find an elephant in our place, among all your mess."

I chuckle through my nose, feeling sad rather than cheerful. I don't know what I did to anger God or whoever runs this universe, but it's unfair that I lose my two best friends in a span of four years.

Hold up, I haven't lost Cara yet!

The muffin piece gets stuck in my throat, and I swallow hard, realizing I'm about to cry.

"You have to come back, Cara," I whisper. "I'm not cleaning your mess or your room. Just saying. So hurry up."

It must be exhaustion or general unease since I took the job, because my mood falls abruptly. A lump forms in my throat, and in seconds I start bawling, sitting in the chair with my head low as my tears fall onto the stupid muffin.

It passes. Everything always does. That's what they say after you lose a loved one. They are wrong. Grief doesn't go away, but it becomes manageable. Many things pass, but not death. That's a pretty permanent state, if you ask my opinion.

Five minutes later, I sniffle and wipe away the tears. My coffee is cold, my cheeks are hot, my head burns, and the self-pity is finally going away.

"Gotta go, babe," I tell Cara. "I'll be back tonight or tomorrow morning."

I walk out, leaving the muffins and coffee on Cara's side table, and the farther I get from her eerily quiet, disinfected room, the more determined I am to get dirt on Rosenberg.

I have to figure him out. He has to pay for what he's done. I might be reckless, but if I quit now and Cara doesn't make it, I'll regret it for the rest of my life.

One more day, I tell myself.

44

NATALIE

"Boss is hungover," says Rosalie as soon as I get to work. "He'll be home all day, sleeping it off. That means anything he wants, every whim, every request should be executed at the speed of light."

She's in her usual humble mood, as if nothing happened.

Julien appears in the kitchen for a brief second, giving Rosalie quick orders. He doesn't look at me, doesn't greet me, like I'm a traitor, though I definitely did the right thing yesterday.

There's a lot of cleaning to do on the back terrace as well as in the mansion's main area after last night's party. Surprisingly, none of the guests stayed overnight. I get it now. Rosenberg is private, though his "private life" has taken on a sinister meaning after what happened yesterday.

"Where's Nick?" I ask.

Rosalie shrugs. "He didn't tell you?"

"Tell me what?"

A smirk appears on her lips. "I thought you two were *friends.*"

That definitely sounds like an innuendo.

"It's his day off," she says.

The fact that he's not around might allow me to approach the boss. I just need to figure out how.

Rosenberg has locked himself in his bedroom, and apparently, he's still feeling feisty, because two hours later, as I clean the main staircase, I hear a muffled angry voice coming from his bedroom upstairs. A moment later, Julien walks out, no emotion on his face when he sees me.

"Mr. Rosenberg wants chicken soup," he says to me while passing by. Like I care what's on Rosenberg's menu. Also, I highly doubt that Rosenberg got all worked up in his bedroom over chicken soup. "Rosalie will prepare it," Julien says without stopping, already at the bottom of the stairs and not bothering to turn. "But he wants you to bring it up."

Oh?

Anxious, I finish steaming the stairs and the second floor and hurry downstairs.

Maybe the predator remembers me? This is an opportunity to slip the stalker's envelope to him. I remind myself to keep a safe distance from him in case he tries something funny with a syringe or who knows what.

When I step into the kitchen, Julien stands with both his palms on the kitchen island, head hanging low.

I stall, startled by the sight. Something is going on. Not that I'd ever sympathize with this guy—screw him. Everyone here is covering up for Rosenberg. There's no redeeming them. However, Julien did cover for me yesterday. Why?

Right now, he looks off. That's not the usual composed Julien I know, and that's another red flag.

Rosalie leans against that same island, her arms crossed over her chest. Her eyes are red and misted with tears.

"What's happening?" I ask, taking slow steps toward them.

Julien pushes off the counter and walks out, the staff entrance door slamming behind him.

"Whoa. What's going on?" I ask, turning to Rosalie, who wipes her eyes and turns away, making herself busy with the carry-out paper bag.

"Something happened?" I ask.

"Yes, bad news about Darla," she says without meeting my eyes.

"How bad?"

"Well, it can't get worse."

The words stun me. Dead? Darla's dead? This should be none of my business. I didn't even know the girl. But I'm thinking about Cara, my brain making a calculation.

Cara was poisoned sometime after Darla. If Darla was in the same condition, the same coma, and now she has died, what does that mean for Cara? The nurse said Cara's improving. Different people fight the same disease in different ways. Darla's outcome is not a warning sign for Cara. And yet, when Rosalie prepares a lunch tray for Rosenberg, my anxiety kicks in like a brushfire. Especially when she instructs me, "Be quick. Don't do anything stupid. If something feels off, if Mr. Rosenberg makes you feel uncomfortable, you tell me."

Today, there's no dancing around the subject—Rosalie's words are a clear warning.

Holding the tray in front of me, my knees weak, I walk up the staff stairs to the second floor. I stop by Rosenberg's room and press my ear to the door.

He's talking, his voice low, almost in a hushed whisper.

"I'll get you the information, I just need a day or two… Yeah, well, I'm tied up at the moment… Things are crazy.

That's an understatement. You just wait, baby. It's going to be huge."

Baby? Does he have a girlfriend? No one ever mentioned that.

"Just have some fucking patience, will you?" he says angrily. "Be a good girl. I have a lot on my plate right now."

For a moment, the room sinks into silence, then he starts talking again, his voice acquiring a seductive growl. "Are you being kinky with me?" A low chuckle follows. "Sit tight, baby, okay?"

When the conversation stops, I swallow hard and finally muster all my courage.

"You've got it, girl," I tell myself and knock on the door.

45

NATALIE

The door swings open abruptly, revealing Geoffrey Rosenberg in a state that would make his fans gasp.

His red hair is a mess. There are dark circles under his eyes. He's wearing a silk robe over his naked body clad only in boxers—thank god at least for those. The stale odor of booze coming from him is so strong that it makes me gag. I wonder if he keeps a secret stash of alcohol in his room.

His expression turns from irritation to approval. "Finally," he blurts. "Come in."

He walks away, making the door almost slam in my face, and I scramble with the tray in my hands to squeeze in.

He throws himself into a chair by the desk, legs spread wide, and motions with his curled finger. "Here."

Again, I'm not sure that chicken soup is what Rosenberg wants right now because his eyes openly rove my body, making me tense in unease. When I approach, he snatches the bottle of coconut water from the tray and gulps half of it like he's been dehydrated for days. A satisfied sigh leaves his mouth, then his face contorts into a capricious mask.

"What is this?" He studies the bottle with disgust. "Tastes like it's already been in someone's mouth."

"Your favorite coconut water, sir," I say as meekly as I can.

"Yeah, not today."

He tosses it onto the desk and motions for me to set the tray down, then rubs his face with both hands.

"Natalia, is it?" he asks and slumps in the chair, legs wide, head cocked. His hairy chest is on full display, and as I steal a glance, I'm surprised to see that his chest hair is not red but light brown.

He studies me up and down with the same distaste he just gave his favorite coconut water. He's definitely not the sober, composed version of Rosenberg.

"Russian background?" he muses.

Seriously?

I nod. Yeah, he's definitely hungover. And he's a piece of work.

His eyes meet mine, and for a second, I'm confused. I swear his eyes were green. Except now they are blue. I must be imagining things.

"I need you to do something," he says and motions to the nightstand. "Bring me my wallet."

"Yes, sir."

Asshole, I think to myself but do what I'm told.

He pulls a hundred-dollar bill out of the wallet I bring him and offers it to me. "I need you to run to a store and grab me a bottle of Jack."

I take the bill hesitantly, my brain reeling at how to go about this.

I told him the other day that I would do anything. Last night wasn't pretty, but I have a feeling the Crypto King, who now looks like an average Joe after a several-day binge, is a lot more talkative when he's lit. Plus, there's one rule in this house that overrides all the rest—you do everything the boss tells you to do.

He notices my momentary hesitation. "No word to anyone, understood?" His gaze on me hardens. "No. One," he mouths. "Be a good girl. Run." He gives me a backward nod, dismissing me. "And make it quick."

To be honest, I'd like to punch him. I'd like to say no, but this might be my only chance to slip the letter into his room. Also, if there's even a remote chance to get to his phone, I'm curious about his social media, texts, and phone calls. And I think I have a perfect plan.

46

NATALIE

"Where are you going?" Rosalie appears out of nowhere, her hands on her hips as she watches me grab my purse out of the locker.

"Running an errand for Mr. Rosenberg."

"What errand?" she demands as I walk past her.

"He asked me confidentially."

"Did you clear it with Julien?"

I pause by the door before exiting and turn to meet her glare. "I don't have to. My boss is Mr. Rosenberg. And I don't want to lose my job for disobeying him. We all want to get paid, right?"

She should know. Everyone here is paranoid about their jobs.

Just like that, I walk out and run right into Julien, who is standing with his hands in his pockets, his face lifted to the sky like he's watching the clouds.

He's not all right. His head turns slowly in my direction, and the expression on his face takes me aback. At this moment, Julien forgets to rearrange his expression into a cold mask and looks as if he is in pain.

I take several steps toward him. "You okay?"

He doesn't answer, only locks eyes with me for the longest time, which unnerves me. He stares at me like this is the last time he'll see me and he's trying to engrave my face in his memory.

His gaze is sad. His features have acquired a handsome softness. On a face that usually looks sharp, it's unusual. I'd give the hundred bucks that I have in my pocket to know what he's thinking.

"Why did you cover for me yesterday?" I ask. "When you said a caterer gave Rosenberg a drink? You lied."

He doesn't answer. Of course he doesn't.

Some people are easy to read. Others are good at masking their emotions. Often, it's because of past trauma, and only booze, drugs, or extreme situations make them open up. Julien is reserved, probably an introvert, but he possesses a peculiar magnetism that's even more intriguing when he reveals so little about himself. An unusual feeling surges through me, a momentary attraction. In different circumstances, I would've flirted with him. In a different place and time, I would've probably made it my mission to get under his skin until all he could think about was me.

These are untimely thoughts. I've known the guy for three days, most of which he's been an ass to me.

"Are you not going to answer?" I ask.

"You shouldn't fraternize at work," he finally says—a rule, of all things.

"I don't."

"That's not what it looked like yesterday."

He means Nick? "I was off my shift. I was going home. That's *outside* work."

"On the premises."

"Jesus, Julien. Really? What? Are you jealous or something?"

A split second of surprise flashes across his face.

I smile. "I'm joking. Obviously."

He looks away, shaking his head. "Why are you so stubborn?" he mutters.

"Do you have siblings?" I ask in return.

He ignores my question again.

"I have two," I say. Not quite true, but I always considered Lindsey and Cara my sisters. "One passed away not long ago. The other one is in critical condition in a hospital. I need money."

That's a simple way to put it, but it will do.

"There are other jobs," Julien replies.

"This is quick money. Maybe I want to splurge and travel to Greece. Or buy a new iPhone. Or invest in crypto." I wiggle my brows.

His jaw tightens—bad joke, I get it. That's probably what Darla was trying to do, schmoozing Rosenberg.

The silence that follows grows even more uncomfortable.

"You want anything from the store?" I ask.

"Are you getting him alcohol?"

The comment startles me. So, it's not the first time Rosenberg has sent someone to secretly get booze, and Julien knows about it.

"Do you need anything?" I repeat, ignoring his question.

He smirks and lowers his eyes. "He could stay drunk in his room for weeks, for all I care."

And that—*that*—doesn't make sense. That's the first rule of the house—no booze. Everyone is concerned about Rosenberg behaving himself because tomorrow is a big day

179

for IxResearch. Yet Julien says *that*? Nothing makes sense today.

I'm about to walk off when Julien calls my name. It sounds gentle, almost caring. "Be careful, okay?"

There's no warning in his voice this time, just concern, and that somehow doesn't make sense either.

Slowly, I bring my fingers to the side of my forehead in a military salute. "Yes, boss," I say, smiling.

Julien shakes his head, turning away, hiding it, but I already caught a smile in his eyes.

I walk to my car, about to get in, when I see someone by the garden shed staring at me. It's Walter, the gardener. He's openly glaring. I have a feeling that he has been watching me since I've been outside with Julien. He and Dave, the security guy, should have a glaring competition.

I wave to Walter, and he turns and stomps away. I haven't really spoken to him at all. I don't think he likes me. I rarely see him inside the house. He's always running errands or doing outdoor stuff. But whenever I see him, his eyes are trained on me like I'm an enemy of the state.

Why do I get all these glares at The Splendors? This place is giving me the creeps, but I really have to figure out Rosenberg.

Booze? *Your wish is my command.*

Except I have a little surprise for Rosenberg. I don't know what game he's playing, but I'm definitely not going to be a pawn. I need him to talk, not fight. I need him to be a teddy bear, not a predator. Today, he won't try anything funny, or at least, he won't be able to. Because I'm going to use his own weapon.

When I get in my car, I open the glove compartment and take out a KitKat. Except when I peel back the wrapper, it reveals a thin rectangular lid. It's one of those diversion "secret stash" products. Inside it—I hope Cara hasn't used it for anything crazy—is a little baggie with pills, Ambien. Cara occasionally takes them at parties to mellow out and chill. Me, I used half of one for sleep, and it knocked me out for twelve hours.

Right now, I need two. When I'm at the store parking lot, away from any possible cameras, I'll grind them into powder and wrap them in the discarded chocolate wrapper I have. When Rosenberg drinks his Jack, he'll drink this too, and then I'll have my way with him.

47

ANONYMOUS

You are supposed to keep this place in check. What do you do? Brood over a girl who can't follow the rules.

   Bravo, Julien!

48

NATALIE

When I return to The Splendors, before I even get out of the car, I do several things.

First, I put the little chocolate wrapper with ground-up sleeping powder in my pants pocket.

Second, I put my phone on silent, turn on the recorder app, and tuck the phone under my shirt and the hem of my pants. Screw the no-phone rule. When I'm upstairs with Rosenberg, I need proof of everything that's being said and done. I wish my breasts were bigger so I could use my bra as a hiding place. Alas.

Next, I take the large cookie tin I got in the store, empty the cookies into a plastic bag, then stick a bottle of Jack Daniel's into it. If I'm on hidden cameras, there's no way to prove there's anything in the tin but cookies.

Last, I need to take the envelope the stalker gave me and stick it in my pocket. I rummage through the stuff in my purse but can't find it. Worried, I dump the contents of the purse onto the passenger seat, feverishly go through all of it, then turn the lining of my purse inside out, but the envelope is nowhere to be seen.

Crap. I definitely put it in my purse this morning before I left my apartment.

My head spins as I give up the useless purse search and lean back against my seat. Someone has gotten into my purse. Someone took the envelope. I don't know what was in it, what type of info, but if it's for Rosenberg's eyes only, it must be sensitive, and whoever took it knows I had it.

Dammit!

Okay, maybe it's in the locker. Maybe it fell out.

I take several deep breaths to calm my nerves, pick up the cookie tin and my purse, and step out of the car.

Just as I approach the staff entrance, the door opens and Walter, the gardener, walks out.

"Hey, Walter," I say, walking past him, but he only stares me down, then loudly spits on the ground.

What's his problem with me?

I cringe and turn around. When I walk in, he's still staring and hasn't moved an inch.

The door closes behind me, but I wait for ten seconds, then slowly open it again and peek outside.

Yep, the weirdo is still standing there, staring in my direction.

"Can I help you?" I ask. "You feeling okay?" *Seriously, dude.*

With painful slowness, Walter squints at the sun, then fixes his baseball hat and, without a word, walks off toward the garden shed.

My friendliness falls off my face as soon as I close the door. I walk to the locker and, first things first, search it for any signs of the envelope.

Nothing.

Nerves bunch in my stomach. There's a minuscule chance that the envelope fell out of my purse back home, in the hallway, but somehow, I don't think that's the case.

"Back so soon?" Rosalie's loud voice behind me makes me jump. She's gotten into the habit of creeping up on me.

"Yes." I shove the purse in the locker and, holding the tin under my arm, walk past her.

"I need you in the kitchen!" Rosalie barks at my back.

"I need to deliver this to the boss," I snap, without turning around.

"What are you delivering?" she insists, though I keep walking.

"It's cookies-and-milk time!" I shout back and turn the corner toward the stairs. I'm done playing the good girl in this house.

Upstairs, I knock on the door.

"Come in!" Rosenberg calls out from inside.

When I walk in, his eyes right away dart to the tin.

"About time. What took you so long?" He walks up and snatches the tin out of my hands, pops the lid, and grunts in satisfaction as he pulls out the bottle. "Smart girl."

Impatiently, he twists the lid off the bottle and takes a greedy gulp.

Yep, he has a problem. And he definitely doesn't care about who I am and what I do as long as I bring him his fix. I have a feeling this bottle will be empty soon.

"Want some?" he offers.

"I don't drink, sir. But I'd be happy to keep you company."

I want to watch his transformation because, as per what I saw yesterday, it's dramatic, to say the least.

His phone beeps with a message, and I take this moment to do what I planned.

"May I?" I reach for the bottle. I already noticed a mini fridge with soft drinks and a shelf with glasses in the opposite corner. "Take a seat and relax. I'll make you a drink."

As I walk to the mini fridge, I look over my shoulder and see Rosenberg arrange himself on the bed, in a half-lying position, his back against the headboard. That's not what I meant by "relax," and I tense at the sight, but right away Rosenberg gets preoccupied with his phone, which works great.

Discreetly, with my back to him, I pull the chocolate wrapper with the powdered drug out of my pocket, empty it into a glass from the shelf, then quickly top it with whiskey.

I turn around and smile, a glass in my hand.

Rosenberg is not paying attention to me. It's all right. I just need him to drink. And if he drinks even half of this, he'll be out in half an hour.

"Sir?" I pass him the drink as I approach.

He greedily snatches it out of my hand, his attention back on the phone, and takes a large gulp. A contented "ahh" escapes him. He smacks his lips. I'm about to ask him a question or two, see if I can get him to talk, when he orders, "Lock the door."

My stomach sinks.

Oh, crap.

49

NATALIE

The words make my spine steel. Rosenberg doesn't look at me to see my reaction, he just keeps scrolling through his phone. I have a feeling that no matter how long I stand, he won't look at me. This guy is used to ordering people around.

I walk to the door and lock it, taking a deep breath to fight the nervousness.

Rosenberg shifts, sitting up, so that there's room between his back and the headboard. Without looking up from his phone, he taps his shoulder with his glass. "I need some work here."

Phew. I almost laugh in relief. This asshole wants a massage?

I hesitate for a second, deciding what to do, then kick off my shoes and get on the bed behind him.

When my hands touch his shoulders—and thank god he didn't remove his robe so there's no skin contact—he grunts, then takes another gulp of his drink.

I cringe, massaging him slowly, meanwhile looking over

his shoulder. He's on social media. I can't see his profile, but he's scrolling through pictures of a model named Mariah Dove. I'm assuming she's a model because she's half naked in most of the pictures—great body, luxury setting.

I keep massaging him, cringing at the fact that I'm sitting on his bed, and that's highly inappropriate. But I keep stealing glances at his phone. Meanwhile, his drink gets emptier. The drug hasn't had enough time to dissolve properly, because this guy chugs booze like air, and soon, he might see the leftover powder on the bottom of the glass.

"Another one?" I ask and, without waiting for a response, take the glass out of his hand, hop off the bed, and go to refill it.

"So, what's the important business deal you have coming up, sir?" I ask when I bring him another drink.

"Shhh. Be quiet," he tells me and keeps scrolling, taking big gulps of his drink until it's empty again, and he passes it back to me.

I continue to massage him and feel his body slightly sagging. The sedative is working, so I try to start a conversation again.

"Tomorrow is an important day for you, isn't it?" I ask carefully.

This time, Rosenberg stiffens.

"Let go," he says curtly, shaking my hands off his shoulders, and turns to face me. "Who sent you?"

My breath hitches in my throat. "Pardon me? I'm just trying to relax you," I murmur, managing a smile and patting the bed. "Why don't you—"

"Who?" Rosenberg snarls, snatching my wrist and leaning forward, his nostrils flaring. This sudden change in him is unsettling, causing my heart to pound. "*He* sent you, didn't he?" His eyes burn with hate. "To test me?" He reaches for me and grabs the back of my neck, yanking me closer. "I was wondering why you were so helpful," he hisses, his face so close that I could get tipsy from his liquor breath.

"N-no, no-no-no. What are you talking about?" I ask, panic rising inside me. As gently as I can, I push his hand away and smile weakly. "I want to make you feel good, sir. You have to take it easy before tomorrow. Why don't you lie down?"

Rosenberg blurts out an angry laugh. "He's trying to get to me, isn't he, fucker?"

Is he talking about the blackmailer? So he knows about him?

"He's always harassing me." Rosenberg fumbles and sloppily lowers himself onto his stomach. "It's okay. I know what I'm doing." He lazily stretches himself out and closes his eyes, muttering, "Eat shit, buddy."

Heart in my throat, I shift to sit next to him and try massaging him, but he stops me. "Do it properly," he slurs, without opening his eyes. "Straddle me and do it the right way."

Not a freaking chance. "Yes, sir, in a second. I'm going to do your neck, loosen it up, then carry on as you please."

I won't. Because I know how the drug works. I was curious about Rosenberg's temper, but it's for the best that it doesn't show. And it won't, because two minutes later, the asshole is fast asleep.

Good.

I wipe my hands on my pants like I just touched something dirty and carefully reach for Rosenberg's phone.

There might be cameras here. If I get caught, I'll say I was curious and bored and was watching him sleep, making sure he's okay. Stupid? For sure. But I can play stupid. Been there, done that. I'll even cuddle up to him while I'm on his phone so I can hide it between us and take pictures of anything I find on it with my own phone and do research later.

Rosenberg's phone is fingerprint-protected, and that's just perfect. I knew that getting into his office computer would be impossible. No one ever has a chance at guessing a password to a stranger's computer unless it's 12345.

But the newest fingerprint protection is great. I gently pick up Rosenberg's motionless hand and press one of his fingers to the phone. The screen lights up.

Excited and petrified at what I might find, I open the photo folder.

There are only twenty or so photos—Rosenberg in a restaurant, with other people, suits, ties, and evening dresses, probably investors, then a photo of the half-naked chick from social media, but this time, it's not a professional shot but a selfie.

And that's it.

Disappointed, I look for any other folders with documents, potentially fingerprint-secured, but there are none.

Huh.

I go to the message folder. The only messages on the phone are from someone called "My Dove," which I assume is the model, and they are all from today. I read the chat, but it's the boring "Miss you," "When do I see you again?" "Want to play?" "How's business?"—mostly from her, whereas Rosenberg responds in curt replies like, "I'll call you soon."

Phone call history—none, except for today's. There are several phone calls from "The Driver." Must be Nick. Another one is from "My Dove."

That's it. The guy freaking cleans his history every day. Who *does* that? Unless they have something to hide. Or they're hiding from someone. Unless... they're up to no good and don't want to get busted.

I open the IxResearch app. Rosenberg's account is fingerprint-protected. I take Rosenberg's hand and press his finger to the square with a prompt.

"Good evening, Mr. Geoffrey Rosenberg!" the screen says and shifts to the dashboard.

But the dashboard is not what I expected.

Crypto wallet—0.

Funds—0.

Trading score—0.

Transactions and invoices—none.

What the hell?

My mind scrambles to make sense of this. Something is very, very wrong with this scenario.

I go to Rosenberg's social media. The first app goes straight to the log-in screen, but when I press Username, it doesn't give me a prompt for the previous usernames used.

I go to the next app—same thing, like he's never used it, or it was reset.

Next one—he's logged in. Bingo! The picture is a black circle, username @JkllnHyde. If this is a reference to Jekyll and Hyde, it's definitely on point. Most people Rosenberg follows are celebrities and notable public figures. His follower count is zero. Posts—zero.

I open a web browser and search the history. There are multiple links, mostly news blogs, but the search history only shows today's activity. Any IT tech could've pulled the scraped info off his phone to see what he deleted. But I'm not a pro.

I thoroughly go through his phone like a detective, checking every download folder, recent files, screenshots, including the caches and trash—nothing. I check the settings and see that the phone is not backed up to any server, doesn't have the sign-in info, not even the service provider log-in.

This man has no trace of anything he's done online. No digital footprint. This is hard to pull off these days. It's especially bizarre because the guy is a genius in the digital world.

And that makes this discovery even more jarring—it looks like Geoffrey Rosenberg is a ghost...

50

ANONYMOUS

A massage? Really? If I didn't know you better, I'd think you were just like Darla. That girl decided she could score some quick money. Now, Darla is dead.

Irritated, I watch you snoop through Rosenberg's phone. You are getting close, Natalie. Too close. You weren't supposed to. Somehow, you managed to find your way into this house at the worst possible time. And you might ruin everything because it's all about to go down...

DAY 5

51

NATALIE

Today is my day off. Alternatively, I might've been let go, but I've yet to find out.

Yesterday, before I left The Splendors, Julien said they wouldn't need me today. I argued. I texted Nick. Nick didn't reply. I called him multiple times but didn't get a response. I gave up, and Julien walked me out to my car after my shift—I guess he finally forced me out.

I still didn't get what I wanted on Rosenberg. I have no choice but to wait for Nick to call back. Maybe I pushed it with sneaking booze to Rosenberg, but I'm pretty sure I can talk Nick into letting me work there longer.

It's Monday, and I try to sleep in, but come seven o'clock, I'm staring at the ceiling above my bed, the thoughts in my head a pack of flies. Eventually, I get up, walk to the living room, and plop myself on the couch.

I'm wearing a tank top and a pair of underwear, the way I usually am, and I have no desire to put on any clothes or do anything. The apartment needs cleaning. I need to run errands. After Julien paid me, I have enough for rent for the next month. I should be grateful, but after working for days, after all the pressure and stress, I feel drained and lonely.

I call the hospital, but there's no update on Cara.

"She might come to any day. Or not." That seems to be the usual answer.

It all depends on her strength, and I pray that she has it. She's always been a strong girl. I will go to see her later, spend some time with her. I've been so caught up with The Splendors job for the last several days that I completely disregarded everyone else. I've ignored calls and texts from friends who were asking about Cara. What do I tell them? To pray for her?

A message dings on my phone—from Cara's boss. She is asking for an update.

There are no updates. One day you have a friend, the next, your friend is in some type of mental purgatory, and the void in your life is an infinite gaping hole. If Cara doesn't pull through, several months will go by, and everyone will forget about her. The world will carry on, just like it did after Lindsey had passed.

Except me.

Even Trixy the Rat is suspiciously quiet today. Maybe she's just happy that I'm finally home.

I bite the inside of my cheek, trying to shoo away the welling tears and the ache in my chest. I play with the phone, twisting it in my hands, when it starts vibrating with the incoming call.

Detective Dupin.

"Yes," I answer.

"Miss Olsen?"

"Yes."

"Detective Dupin here. How are you?"

I'm sure she didn't call for small talk. "Did you look into Geoffrey Rosenberg?"

"We have, we have." She clears her throat, her tone not reassuring at all. "This is a complicated matter, you see. Geoffrey Rosenberg is a very high-profile man."

Why am I not surprised that she's started the conversation with that exact statement?

"He is well-connected and not easy to reach," she continues.

"Did you *try* to reach him?"

"Anything that has to do with Mr. Rosenberg goes through his lawyers. Right now, we have absolutely no evidence of his connection to your friend. Nothing less than a legal summons will work with a man like him."

I curse to myself—I knew it from the start.

"The fact that your friend left the club with him doesn't prove his involvement," the detective continues.

"What about the other girl? The one I told you about?"

"I didn't find a record of any admission to any local hospitals or New York City hospitals. Not with those symptoms."

I chew on my lip, swallowing my anger at Julien. Did he lie? Everyone at The Splendors lies and cheats and commits crimes that go unpunished.

"So what do we do about him?" I ask.

The hesitation from Detective Dupin gives me a clear answer.

"Nothing?" I say at the same time the detective says, "Nothing."

"I figured," I say bitterly. Nothing is happening, and nothing will happen. "What now?"

"Where are you right now?"

"Home. It's my day off."

"You are not planning on going back, are you?"

"Goodbye, Detective," I say sharply, hang up, and toss my phone onto the table.

Once again, the silence in the apartment is depressing.

I should turn on Spotify, but Cara has always been in charge of the music choice. Strange how you take for granted the smallest things your roommate does for you. Until she's gone, and the realization kicks in that the choice of your breakfast muffins' flavor wasn't in fact yours, and you are not sure where she put the laundry detergent the last time she used it, and you need to send the rent money to the landlord, but she was the one who used to do the cash transfers, so you don't even know the landlord's email.

This is so way past music and muffin choices.

Cara doesn't talk to her parents much, not after the big Thanksgiving fight they had two years ago. But I probably should inform them what's happened to her. Though, to be fair, if she comes to and finds them next to her hospital bed, she'll probably flip out. We, small-town folks, keep our small-town past an arm's length away from our New York City life.

I lower my face into my hands and take a deep breath, trying to hold myself together.

What was the point of the last nine years?

When we ended up in the big city, only nineteen, broke but full of hopes, we learned to hustle. We picked up random jobs. We graduated college, and by then, we upgraded to upscale workplaces, learned the ins and outs of the big city, made friends, partied, went through multiple heartbreaks, tried nine-to-five jobs, quit, went to tipping jobs because the misery of nine-to-five didn't justify our fancy college degrees. We wanted to experience life, party, have it all. We saw the rich and the poor, and the rich hadn't necessarily gotten to where they were because of a college degree. We thought we could screw up and start again. We took risky chances and made questionable decisions. Because we were young, pretty, and invincible. Or so we thought.

Until our smartest friend died of cancer.

Until my prettiest and most talented one ended up in a hospital with "little brain activity."

And my world as I knew it came to a halt.

My melancholia gives way to anger, slow and thick, getting thicker by the second. That anger pushes away the sadness and Trixy's annoying scratching at the metal cage bars.

"Nope. Not today," I tell myself. "I won't just fold and wait for what's to come."

I might've screwed up yesterday by losing the letter, but it looks like the stalker guy is my only way to nail Rosenberg. Cara deserves this revenge.

I open the laptop on the coffee table and power it up. I search the web for the free apps to call a number from a computer. If I can't use my phone, that should do it.

When I press the Connect button, the phone receiver emoji on the screen starts jiggling. Three rings into it, the guy picks up.

"This is Natalie," I say right away.

There's a pause. I wonder if he's trying to remember who I am.

"I'm working for Geoffrey Rosenberg, remember?" I jolt his memory.

"Where are you calling from?"

"It's an app on my computer."

"I told you not to call me from home," he hisses.

"It's an app. Untraceable, right?"

"Your fucking IP address is traceable!"

I'm pretty sure he calls me something inappropriate under his breath.

"Why are you home?" he snaps.

"Day off," I snap back.

"You got that letter to Rosenberg?"

I can't tell him that it might've been stolen by someone at the mansion. "No. I lost it."

"You *what*?"

"By accident. We need another plan."

A row of curses follows. "Listen. Don't call me from home, your home computer, or anything like that. I don't want to be tracked."

I roll my eyes.

"Let's meet," he says curtly. "Jersey City. The gas station on West Side Ave. One o'clock. Don't be late."

"How am I—"

The audio bubble on the screen bursts, indicating the end of the phone call.

52

NATALIE

Five minutes to one, I pull into the gas station on West Side Avenue.

No matter which radio channel I tune to, the talk shows go on and on about today's news.

"Are you ready, you little crypto junkies? Ready for the big splash? Today, IxResearch goes public," a radio DJ announces in an overly excited voice. "You know what that means? It means that if you reserved your I-X market shares, in a matter of days, you'll be raking in profit. If you didn't buy the shares yet, don't walk. Run! Now!"

I kill the radio. If I hear the words "crypto" or "IxResearch" one more time, I'm going to throw up.

The gas station is busy. *Good.* The stalker guy might be a psycho or a criminal. You can never be too careful. I tell the gas station attendant to pump regular, step out of my car, and stand by its rear, my arms crossed over my chest.

I study every car, every person walking in and out of the

convenience store. Still, the guy manages to sneak up on me, approaching from behind the gas pump.

"Natalie?"

His voice whips me around.

He seems normal. His regular height, a plain middle-aged face, jeans, tie-dye T-shirt, and baseball hat make him look so phenomenally average that I wouldn't have recognized him even if I had met him before a dozen times.

Hands in his pockets, he looks around, scanning the gas station. He could be holding a knife in his pocket or some other weapon, though there's no reason for him to hurt me. Besides, that's the freaking problem with my curiosity—it's a professional habit. I want to know more about Rosenberg, and nothing is more intriguing than this guy's words from several days ago about going to the police.

So I keep a straight face.

"You alone?" he asks, still scanning the place like he's on the run.

"Yes."

"Let's go," he says. Without waiting for my reply, he gets into the passenger seat of my car.

I give the attendant a twenty, get in the driver's seat, and turn to look at the guy.

Inside the car, his presence is far more intimidating.

"Talk," I say.

"Let's go somewhere else."

"Nah. Nuh-huh. I don't even know what this is about. I don't need any more trouble. Someone has already searched my place, and now you want me to put you in touch with the man who doesn't want to deal with you."

Grunting in irritation, he throws his head back against

the seat. "I'll pay you. Like I said, it will be beneficial for both of us."

"Beneficial? Which part? A restraining order? No, thank you."

His eyes snap to me. "Don't be stupid," he grits out, his expression shifting several degrees closer to psychotic.

I lean away from him. "Excuse me?"

"Listen," he says urgently, ducking his head and thievishly looking through the windows. "You can make money on this. Trust me. I will explain."

"Make money how? You still haven't told me what it's about."

"Aha! Curious?" He lights up. "There's a lot of money in that house."

"Yeah. And I'm not a thief."

"Your boss is."

That gets my attention.

He nods, noticing my surprise. His eyes narrow with a mischievous smile. "Your boss is a fraud. I know for a fact, and I'll tell you all about it. Five minutes." He looks around again. "Ten tops. Twenty max."

"I can see that you already started negotiating."

He chuckles, his cautious look replaced by an arrogant one. "You have no idea, sweetheart. This is in both of our interests." He motions with his fingers. "Let's go."

I do a quick evaluation of the scenario. The gas station is busy. There's a camera on the parking lot. We are in the middle of Jersey City, so we will be driving on main streets. There's nothing this guy can do to hurt me. And why would he?

"Any public place will do," he says, noticing my hesitation. "Public places are good. A café or something." His eyes dart around, scanning the parking lot. "I'd rather not be inside the car, yours or mine, in case…"

"In case of what?" If I thought I was paranoid, this guy definitely one-ups me.

He motions with his finger near his ear. "In case someone is listening."

"You gotta be kidding me."

He shakes his head. "You really are clueless, aren't you?"

"Whatever. Let's go," I say, determined. Now I really need to hear what he has to say. A public place is perfect. "What do you mean by fraud? How's Rosenberg a fraud?" I ask as I pull out of the gas station and onto the street.

"Go, go, go," he hurries me, looking around like he's being followed. "They might be watching."

Again, I have no idea who "they" are, but I'm determined to find out.

53

NATALIE

Paranoid is an understatement. I already know that Rosenberg doesn't have anything on his phone. Not just any work info but anything any normal individual has, so that's suspicious. This stalker guy acts like a classic psycho, but his words start making sense.

"Go to Central and Manhattan Avenue. There's a Colombian coffee shop on the corner," he says, typing away on his phone while I'm driving. "My name is Rich, by the way."

Rich doesn't look quite like a crazy man, though he might be dangerous. But let me tell you something about Jersey City—it's hard to get kidnapped when the heavy traffic doesn't let you move faster than one mile per hour and there are cameras on every intersection and business building.

From time to time, Rich glances up from his phone, and when we approach the destination, he points at the empty parking spot. "Here is good."

Inside the café, he orders a cappuccino, I order an

espresso, and we take seats at a table by the window. While he's typing away on his phone, I study his shaggy black hair under the baseball hat, his several-day stubble, and his worn-out clothes—he's just an average guy in the city.

He finally sets the phone aside, looks over his shoulder, out the window, then returns his cocky stare to me.

"So…?" I prompt. "I didn't come here for coffee."

He leans forward with his elbows on the table. "So, your boss is a thief," he says with a satisfied smug face.

"And you know that how?"

"The asshole owes me money but avoids me like the plague."

"Rosenberg?" I chuckle. "Owes *you*?"

"Uh-huh." His expression gets even more arrogant.

I give him a backward nod. "Owes you for what?"

"Gambling debt."

I snort. "That's ridiculous. He has more money than god. Why would he owe for gambling?"

"That's the problem. He knows that, but I can't seem to get ahold of him. He's like a weasel. That gig got into his head."

"A gig?"

I should probably walk out right now, considering this psycho calls the crypto millionaire's career a *gig*, but Rich continues.

"He won't talk to me. Won't see me. Won't pay me back. Except now, his debt has grown interest."

"How much are we talking about?"

"It's not a matter of how much he owes me, but how much I'm asking for."

"And that is?"

"Twenty million."

I choke in shock. "Holy crap!"

Rich smirks and leans back in his chair.

"And why would Geoffrey Rosenberg pay you that?" I ask.

"Because otherwise, I'll tell everyone about Phil Crain."

I scrunch up my brows. "Who is Phil Crain?"

Rich drapes his arm behind the chair back and runs his tongue inside his bottom lip, then sucks his teeth loudly and with visible satisfaction.

"All right." I roll my eyes in annoyance. "Are you talking in parables? Clues? I don't have time for freaking *Jeopardy!*"

Rich leans on the table to bring his face closer to mine.

"Phil Crain," he says slowly, "is an alcoholic and a gambler."

"I still don't understand."

Rich's lopsided grin grows when he adds, "Who is now pretending to be Geoffrey Rosenberg."

54

NATALIE

It takes me a moment to process Rich's words. Not the twenty million, but the fact that Rosenberg is a fake.

Rich studies me expectantly, enjoying the effect of his words. "See what I'm saying? If you help me get to him, I'll pay you. After I get the money, of course."

"You seem quite sure that you will get it."

He shoots me a look. "Oh, I will. You think I'm just ripping on some rich guy for no reason?"

"Obviously, luck is not on your side."

"I didn't get a chance to talk to him. He's always either in the mansion, which is secured, or with his driver, who doesn't let anyone get close. I sent a letter."

I snort. "You kidding me? A letter?"

"What's wrong with a letter?" His expression hardens. "I don't think he got it. Because if he did, he'd be *very concerned*."

"Who even sends letters these days? Did you try his email?"

"Several of his business emails. None answered."

"Cell phone?"

"No luck so far. I've gotten one number of his, but my messages go unanswered."

I have a feeling that this guy might be delusional or a scam artist after all. But then, maybe that's what Rosenberg was talking about yesterday when he got drunk.

"Maybe he doesn't care?" I suggest.

"The guy knows that he is an impostor."

"And no one else knows?"

"Well, he's being stupidly open lately. His face was on the cover of *Tech Weekly*."

"And you read that sort of stuff or something?"

"Nah. But I know Phil when I see him, even with the dyed hair and makeup and all that stuff."

"And you know him how?" I probe.

Rich shakes his head, irritated, then looks around the café like a thief.

"Listen here." He beckons me closer, and I lean in, going along with him for now. "If you're trying to get intel here, it won't work. That's *my* gig. *My* money, okay? But I'm willing to share. You want a payday, sweetheart, you do exactly what I tell you. Unless you want to end up like the others."

The comment jolts me upright. "Excuse me?"

This sounds like a direct warning.

His phone makes a weird honking sound, which I assume is a notification. Suddenly, Rich's eyes widen at the screen so dramatically that they appear ready to fall out of their sockets.

"Oh, shit." His amused chuckle sounds like a screech. "Will you look at that."

Why do I have a feeling that this guy has a list of blackmail options?

Rich clicks his tongue. "Payday!" His face lights up, and he gets up abruptly, almost knocking his chair backward. "There come my twenty million," he says with a satisfied grin. "I don't need you. Ciao." He starts walking away but pauses at the door and turns around. "Oh!" He nods at me. "I suggest staying away from that mansion."

In a second, he's out the door, like he's never been here.

I sit dumbfounded.

What was that about twenty million? Does that mean that Rosenberg messaged him back? And now this soon-to-be-rich douchebag doesn't need me?

The questions keep swirling in my head as I wave off the cashier who's motioning for the coffees that are ready. I dart outside. I want to know more. I want to know if the twenty million he just brought up are actually coming from Rosenberg and if Rich is still going to give me the inside information he promised.

Suddenly, a loud honking sound and the screech of tires slice through the air. A loud scream follows. A man in a black hoodie, jeans, and blue sneakers darts away from the intersection and disappears around the corner.

The sounds of multiple cars braking and honking fill the street.

Someone shouts, "Help!"

Rich is nowhere in sight, but people start trotting toward the intersection, a crowd gathering fast, and I make my way toward it, curious, looking over others' shoulders to see what happened.

"He walked right out," someone says.

"He got pushed," someone else suggests.

"Yeah, there was someone behind him."

"That guy with blue sports sneakers, where did he go?"

"The ambulance is on the way."

"He's dead, definitely dead."

A van stands sideways in the middle of the road, blocking traffic. My eyes catch sight of the body splayed on the pavement in front of it, the legs and arms contorted in an unnatural way. The head is turned to the side, and the growing pool of blood under it is jarring—the guy is definitely dead.

I feel bile gathering in my throat—not just any guy. It's Rich.

55

NATALIE

I'm staring at the dead man, fear gripping me as the crowd thickens.

"Didn't he just come out of the coffee shop?" someone asks.

"Yeah! He was there with someone. I saw him through the window."

I can't be here. Rich was a blackmailer, and he just told me that Rosenberg is a fraud, told me that right before the accident. Or was it murder?

The sound of police sirens approaching is my warning sign.

Dread coils inside me. I frantically search for my car, but it's blocked off by the stalled traffic.

My eyes meet those of one of the bystanders. He frowns at me, taking a step in my direction. "Didn't you just come out of the coffee shop?" he asks, pointing at me.

My knees go weak. I can't get involved. If I talk to the police, the investigation will start. I'll have to mention

Rosenberg, The Splendors, and Rich's blackmailing plan. What if Rich was right, and now I'm the only person who knows that Rosenberg is a fake? If I talk to the police, the moment I walk out of the police station, I am a witness, and that means...the next target.

The thoughts spin in my head with the speed of a tornado, and when several police cars pull up at the scene of the accident, I stumble backward, then turn around and start running.

I run in an unknown direction. It doesn't matter where, as long as it's far away from the dead body. Rich's words pound in my head with every step—what if *they* are watching me? Have *they* been watching me this whole time? What if *they* saw me with Rich?

Fear clogs my throat, making it hard to breathe. I feel like I'm choking. I can't think straight, but I keep running. I should've run from The Splendors as soon as I discovered the first hidden camera. But no—I walked into the trap of my own will, doo-dee-doo, thinking I was so clever, playing with the sharks.

I'm so angry at myself! I need to disappear, take a vacation, leave town. Except I don't have much money. I can't leave Cara behind. And there's not a single person I can talk to. Except maybe...Nick.

I pull out my phone and frantically dial his number.

"Hey, doll," he answers. His voice is cheerful and calm, in contrast to my wildly beating heart. "How's work?"

"Nick, I'm not at work. We need to meet up."

"Are we talking about a date?" He chuckles.

God, I wish I was in the mood for flirting. "Something serious. Very serious."

"You okay?" he asks, his voice growing concerned.

"I'm not sure."

"Natalie, what's up? Are you at The Splendors?"

"No. Something's come up. Nick, I think you need to get out of that house."

"Whoa, whoa. What's going on? Where are you?"

"Jersey City. Off Central Ave, crossing Griffith."

"Calm down, okay? You're not making sense."

"Nick, please. Can we meet?"

"I'll pick you up. How about in ten minutes? We'll talk. You'll tell me everything."

"Sounds good. Thanks, Nick."

Ten minutes later, Nick's car pulls up to the curb in front of me. The passenger window slides down, and Nick beams at me from his seat. "Hello, trouble."

He studies me with curiosity as I settle in the passenger seat, then starts driving.

I close my eyes and take a deep breath, trying to calm my heartbeat. "I don't know what I got myself into."

"What's going on?"

"I just met with this guy, Rich, who knows Rosenberg." I open my eyes and turn to Nick. "Did the security guards at The Splendors ever tell you about the intruder they were chasing outside the gate several days ago?"

Nick frowns, and I start telling him about the letters and phone calls from Rich—everything Rich told me in the café. When I finally tell him that Rosenberg might be operating under a false identity, Nick shakes his head, his smile gone.

"That sounds wild," he says. "That sounds… Well, that actually sounds like a blackmail plan."

"But I think Rich was right!" I insist.

I know he was. I've had suspicions about Rosenberg for a while. He might just be a bigger monster than I thought.

"Rich is dead, Nick. Do you realize that? And if Rich was right, we might all be in danger."

Nick's phone on the console rings, the name Geoffrey Rosenberg flashing on the screen.

"Yes," Nick answers, his voice low and cautious. Maybe he believes me after all.

I study the car interior, trying to listen in to what the boss says on the other end, but all I hear is his escalated tone, though I can't figure out what it's about. An unusual object in the console attracts my attention—a breathalyzer. That's taking sobriety up a notch.

"Doesn't matter," Nick snaps into the phone, and I tense at the words. "All you have to worry about is the board meeting today. No... Not a problem. Not anymore," he grits out, making my hair stand on end. His voice has acquired a sharp undertone, and it sounds off. "I'm dealing with something right now."

Without saying anything else, he cuts the call and tosses the phone into the console.

I hold my breath. That couldn't have been Geoffrey Rosenberg, right? I've never heard Nick talk in this manner, let alone to our boss.

Abruptly, Nick swerves the car to the curb and parks.

"Why did we pull over here?" I ask, looking out the window to see that we are parked on a very quiet dead-end residential street.

Nick raises himself slightly, trying to get something out of his jeans pocket. Only now do I notice that he's not dressed in his usual suit and tie. He's wearing a T-shirt and jeans. My eyes drop lower, to his shoes, and my breath hitches in my throat—blue, he's wearing blue sports sneakers!

He got pushed.

"Yeah, there was someone behind him."

"That guy with blue sports sneakers, where did he go?"

My blood turns icy cold as I see what Nick pulls out of his pocket. It's an elongated red cartridge, just like the one I found on the floor of the library.

"Nick?" a petrified whisper leaves my mouth.

He turns toward me, his face completely blank. "Seriously, Natalie."

Before I get a chance to say anything else, he lunges at me. A sharp stab in my neck makes me yelp. When Nick lets go, I frantically pull the door handle, but it won't budge.

Suddenly, my body goes limp, warmth spreading through it, but not a pleasant one—it's paralyzing. I try to say something, but the jumble of words coming out of my mouth is slurred. A wave of nausea washes over me. Everything starts spinning.

Nick caps the cartridge and tosses it into the console, then mutters a curse.

His voice trails off, his last words, "You should've minded your own business."

56

ANONYMOUS

Dammit! Dammit! Dammit!

That's not how it was supposed to go!

Everything seems to be spiraling out of control. I always have a plan B. This? This is plan C. Or D? I've lost count. This has been a long game. I need to finish this, whatever it takes.

No rules.

No mercy.

Knives out.

At this point, nothing is off limits. Not even murder.

57

NATALIE

When I open my eyes, all I see is beige carpeting. It's dim. The brightest spot is the rectangular shape of an open door-way that leads into a large room.

I'm lying on the floor.

The sound of footsteps somewhere means I'm not alone, but when I move to see what's happening, my body doesn't listen. Shaking my head helps my vision to focus just a tad, but my body still won't obey. Then I feel it—the restraints, something holding my wrists and ankles. I make an effort to move, but that only makes them cut deeper into my skin.

I whimper, but something clogs my mouth—a gag.

I try to search my foggy memory for the last thing I remember.

Café. Rich. Accident. Nick. Car ride.

Car ride with Nick! He injected me with something!

The footsteps approach, and familiar blue sneakers appear in front of me. I look up and see Nick staring down at me.

"You are awake. Good."

Nick sits down on his haunches and yanks the cloth out of my mouth.

"Wh-wha—" I swallow hard and lick my lips, trying to unwind my tongue.

"You know," he says, "I didn't take you for a sneaky one. Adventurous, yes. Hardworking—maybe. Smart—doubtful. After all, you can't even follow simple rules."

His spiteful words don't match the charming smile that used to be permanent on his lips, now gone.

"But sneaky?" he continues. "Didn't see that coming. I thought you'd be a mediocre gold digger at best. But look at you, you managed to get tied up with that lowlife, Rich."

"I didn't," I mumble slowly. "I don't—"

He grabs my jaw with his hand, and his fingers dig into my cheeks so hard that I wince and whimper, feeling my molars being crushed by the force. For a moment, the world goes dark as the sharp pain takes over, then Nick pushes my face away from him.

"I don't need to hear what you have to say. Yet," he spits out. "The less you lie, the easier I will make this for you."

His sudden violence is shocking. Another whimper leaves my mouth. I move my jaw, trying to process the pain, as my eyes burn with tears.

Nick gives me a menacing smile. The dreadful realization washes over me—he's a psychopath. He's enjoying this.

"Now, the question is…" He sucks his teeth, studying me. "Red pill or blue pill?"

I frown, not understanding. Is that a reference to *The Matrix*? Harsh truth or blissful ignorance?

"What does that mean?" I ask in a half whisper.

He reaches into his pocket and pulls out two cartridges, red and blue.

My senses slowly start coming back, and with them, dread at the sight of the syringe cartridges. The red one is something mild that he used on me in the car. The other one is what he probably used on Cara and Darla. That means—

"You are figuring it out, aren't you, doll?" Nick smirks. "This"—he picks out the red one—"will make you go night-night for some time again. I have an important board meeting today, then I'll deal with you."

I swallow hard, staring at the blue cartridge. Nick notices and raises it in the air like he's offering candy to a little girl.

"This"—the corners of his lips curl downward—"will affect your nervous system and brain, so *if* you ever wake up, you'll be lucky if you remember your name."

Oh, god... "Is that what you gave Cara?" I snap, and he frowns. "The one who went home with Rosenberg last week?"

His expression becomes suddenly concerned. "Oh, that's interesting. If that's the slut from the club, then she must've gotten the blue one. She said some things she shouldn't have. We have a reputation to protect here. Now, you, on the other hand..." He brings the blue cartridge close to my face and taps my nose with it.

"Please, don't," I beg. "I'll be quiet as a mouse. I'll leave town. I'll go away—"

"You will."

He leans closer.

I try to shift back, farther away from him. "Nick, please," I beg and shake my head. "You don't have to do this. Whatever Rosenberg did, you are not part of it. It's not your fault. I won't tell anyone. You are—"

He slaps my face so hard that my head hits the floor. I gasp and hold my breath, trying to fight the pain and dizziness.

Nick's harsh words pulsate in my head as he speaks. "You should've minded your own business. There's no chance you are getting out of this alive, doll. You understand, don't you?"

His low chuckle makes my eyes snap open, tears blurring his cruel features.

"Please," I beg.

"I'm curious how much you've uncovered," he says. "That's the only reason I'm letting you stay alive for anoth-er"—he checks his wristwatch—"until tonight, I guess."

His phone rings. He fishes it out of his pocket and grunts. "Moron," he mutters and clenches his jaw but doesn't pick up. His gaze slowly slides up my body. "Unfortunately, I have to cut our date short. You just so happen to be sitting on a very sensitive asset. So guard it with your life." He pouts his lips in playful pity. "My little feisty dragon guarding the trea-sure," he coos.

Huh?

He reaches for my face and slowly drags his finger from my chin, down my body, giving my thigh a casual pat.

I clench my teeth in disgust.

"I do want to know what else you found out in this house," Nick says. "As well as who else you told about this. But that will have to be when I come back. Right now, you are getting a very small dose of the red pill."

"No-no-no-no. Please," I beg.

"I need you quiet for the foreseeable future. Even though no one will hear you here anyway."

"Where are we?" I choke out.

"Home, doll, home."

He studies me with some sardonic amusement as he twirls the red cartridge between his fingers, then pops the top off and rearranges it for a stab.

"Please, don't," I beg, trying to appeal to his better judgment.

"Oh." He pauses suddenly. "Out of curiosity, for when the time comes, which will have to be soon. What would you prefer? Suicide? Or your body wrapped in a blanket, stuffed in a trash bag, and buried in a landfill?"

Anger and despair rise in me like a tide. "You…" I start thrashing on the floor, pointlessly trying to yank my hands out of the restraints.

Nick laughs in my face, the sound of it chilling. Then he fists the hair at the back of my head and brings my face close to his. The pain of a hundred needles prickling my scalp makes me gasp, but he tightens his hold on my hair even more.

The only rebellion I can manage is a loud spit in his face.

His smile vanishes. Pure hate flickers in his eyes. "I guess you belong in the trash, doll. You shouldn't have come here."

The stab of the syringe feels slightly familiar. The warmth starts spreading through my body, numbing it.

Stupid. I'm so, so stupid.

Nick puts the gag back in my mouth and shuts the door, leaving me in complete darkness.

Fear grips me. Nausea from the drug washes over me. A sickening thought pulsates in my head—I'm not going to make it, after all.

But that's not what makes my chest shake in helpless sobs. It's the images of my favorite girls in my head.

Hey, Linds-babe. Look who is about to join the party?

Sorry, Cara-babe. I tried. Have all the muffins you can for me. Love you.

58

NICK

Another amateur sticking her nose in my business.

Argh!

The numbers are piling up lately.

I should've checked Natalie's background, but I didn't think much of her.

The only reason I used the mild sedative on her instead of the nerve agent is because I need to know who she's talked to, if she has. I can't keep up with all the conniving bitches who are always swarming around Phil, a.k.a. Rosenberg.

First, there were all those low-level women Phil hooked up with when we first moved into the mansion. With his designer suit and watch, he is a clear prize for any girl who has the wits for this sort of thing. Manhattan is full of opportunistic sluts who raise their tails at the sight of money. Phil is allowed to bring women over, but he can only keep up the act when sober.

When drunk, the dipshit can't keep his mouth shut, blabbering about his past, his future, and the crypto he knows nothing about. So, those gold diggers who got a whiff of something shady had to go away for good. Of course, right away, more came, ready to spread their legs for a potential billionaire.

Then, that housekeeper, Darla, started secretly sleeping with Phil and got drunk with him. He blabbered too much, like the ignorant boastful peacock that he is. He called himself Phil. Obviously, she had to go. The nerve agent always works well. It's expensive, and I really hate to waste it on all the trash.

There was the girl from the club. It puzzles me that Natalie knows about her.

Then there was Rich, who started sending threatening notes. Careless move, too. At first, I thought he was just another lowlife hoping to get rich off random blackmail. He wasn't clear about what he knew until his last message came with the photograph of Phil Crain and a line on the bottom, Phil Crain or Geoffrey Rosenberg? $20,000,000.

Ambitious. Also, immature. He thought a burner phone would disguise his whereabouts. I swindle millions in cash and thousands of investors, and the idiot thought he was the smarter one.

I baited him. I didn't expect him to be in a café, talking to—surprise, surprise—our Natalie.

Another one down. One more to go.

This is getting annoying. The cleanup takes more effort than it should. And all because this low-grade actor from off Broadway can't keep up with his role.

I lock up the closet with Natalie inside just as my phone rings again.

Geoffrey Rosenberg, says the caller ID.

This guy is getting on my nerves, but I need him for at least another day.

"About fucking time," I blurt into the phone when I pick up. "Get ready. Get dressed. Wear your best suit. Best face. You'd better not mess up this meeting. If the breathalyzer shows even a teeny-tiny amount of alcohol in your system, I'm going to kill you, I swear. I need you sharp as a needle."

"I'm fine! I'm fine! I'm ready!" Phil mumbles.

"I'm fine," I mimic him with annoyance. "Better be fine."

"I'm good. Sorry for the last two days. I was under a lot of stress."

"Yeah, well, this is the wrong time for your fuckups. You don't have to do a damn thing besides look smart. I know that's a chore but keep your little brain alert. It's in your best interest."

"I'm working hard here, Nick."

I close my eyes, wanting to punch him in the face. I would've if he were here. Actually, no, I wouldn't have. I would've cracked his ribs. I did once, when he pissed me off by disappearing and binging for three days straight while we were supposed to do an online World Digital Forum presentation.

I'm so tired of that imbecile. He's a mediocre actor and a pathetic person. The only reason he got this gig is pure luck and his uncanny resemblance to the actual Rosenberg. And the actual one? May his soul rest in peace in the backyard of a summer cabin in Vermont. The twenty-first century is all about the survival of the fittest, and the real Geoffrey Rosenberg didn't make the cut.

59

NICK

I picked up Phil Crain when he was drunk as a skunk, in tears, telling the bartender at an Irish pub on the Lower East Side of Manhattan his sad life story. His sniffles were ruining my lunch, but one look at him gave me whiplash. Despite his blond hair and blue eyes, I swear he looked like Rosenberg's doppelgänger. He just needed several tweaks to play the part—red hair dye, green eye lenses, expensive suit, proper attitude. I paid off his gambling debt, promised him a fortune for playing the best role in his life—he was an actor at some shitty off-Broadway place. I should've known he had more debt than he led me to believe. The guy can't keep his life straight.

It's been over a year with this parasite, and I'm about done with him. He thinks he'll get a hefty paycheck, fake passport, and disappear to some South American paradise. As if I could trust an idiot like him. In a couple of days, he will be brain dead in a hospital.

"Listen to me," I tell Phil on the phone. "You get ready,

put on the outfit I chose for you, and read the document I sent you. I don't want you to say anything stupid or sound like a moron in front of our biggest investors. I'll pick you up in twenty. Not a drop of booze, you got me?"

"Jesus, I already told you—"

"Shut! The fuck! Up!" I snap. "Get to work on that document. Practice like it's the most important audition of your life. It *is*, by the way."

I cut the call and grunt in frustration.

He's not any better than the actual Geoffrey Rosenberg. Now, *that* guy was a genius, though also a doormat. I met him several years ago when he was working on a new online digital currency marketplace, which was brilliant, by the way. But he was a lousy networker, so he couldn't find investors. An introvert, a loner, a weirdo—he should've listened to me and made a deal that day three years ago. Could've been still alive.

I had developed a new cryptocurrency, ErFi—nothing special, but big potential if played right. I'd just dumped my investment company, which was a fraud, and got away with a hefty eight figures in my offshore account.

I believe that everything happens for a reason. I lived under a new identity, came to Rosenberg to offer him a collaboration. I don't know if he simply didn't like me or was too protective of his idealistic vision about his online baby, IxResearch. It didn't matter. I wanted my hand in it, but he was stalling.

The evening he and I had an argument at his place, I didn't mean to start a fight. If he'd kept his mouth shut, things would've turned out differently. But he kept on blabbering and blabbering, calling me a fraud, until I punched him in the face.

I know, I know, I have occasional spurts of anger. That one resulted in him falling, hitting his head against the edge of the table, and—

Well, let's just say that a dead body can be a nuisance if you don't know how to dispose of it. Luckily, I had a perfect place, a remote cabin in Vermont that belonged to my grandparents' friend who never used it.

Rosenberg being a recluse worked out fantastically for me. I had access to everything he owned—his apartment, his computers, his software. He didn't have any friends. No family or relatives, his single mom long dead. No one was looking for him. I realized that it would be easy to continue with his project, feeding my own obscure ErFi Coin into his new digital market.

No one knew that Rosenberg was dead. He didn't have to be. But soon, I needed a face for IxResearch and a person who could take all the blame for it later on.

I've been working on this for three years. A year and a half ago, I found that doofus, Phil. It was time to take that enterprise up a notch. I didn't expect it to explode like it did, with the company's net worth skyrocketing to almost a billion.

I could've kept it up for longer. If it were mine, that is. Unfortunately, there's too much mess with Rosenberg's identity, so that will have to play out differently.

Today is a big day. The company is officially going public and releasing the shares onto the stock market. With the raging interest from the investors, it's only a matter of days until the stock prices soar. I'll transfer the rest of the IxResearch investments to my offshore accounts, and bye-bye! The thousands of idiots who invested in yet another crypto venture will be bankrupt. Serves them right. Bernie

Madoff will pale in comparison, but unlike him, when the feds get a whiff of what's happening, I'll be across the world, sipping cocktails on the beach under a new identity.

60

NICK

I sit down at the desk and turn on the computer screens.

Here it is, my empire at a glance.

There are three computers at my place. It's a joke calling this guest house at the back of The Splendors "my place," but I had to keep a low profile, all the while living close to that imbecile, Phil, to curate his daily life and keep up the charade. That turned out to be harder than building a billion-dollar business. Stupid people should be lobotomized. But then I wouldn't have my business.

I'm about done playing the driver. Trying to be humble. Smiling like a good boy. Following orders in public while wanting to cave in Phil's face. Acting like I'm one of the staff, one of those gray mice who day to day clean other people's mess.

Phil *truly* believes that playing Rosenberg is the biggest acting role of his life. It probably is, considering he'll be dead as soon as I'm done with him.

I check the latest transfer of partial funds from IxResearch to one of my offshore accounts. That's another ten million dollars. I launder in increments. I have over a dozen separate accounts all around the world, in the "gray list" countries that are tax havens.

I check the ErFi market price and smile in satisfaction—my baby is growing, gaining popularity thanks to IxResearch.

I look at my watch—Rosenberg should be ready by now. I log out of all the computers and check the house cameras on my phone. There are six. I don't have cameras in the office, library, or any of the bedrooms, as per Phil's plea for privacy, but I see him already walking downstairs and into the living room.

Good. He can wait.

I take a quick shower and put on my best suit. Yes, I'm a driver, but at important meetings, I serve as Rosenberg's assistant. Looking sharp is the best representation of a team.

"Looking fine, Eric," I tell myself in the mirror, fixing my tie. I might stick with Nick for a while. I like that alias, but I miss my actual name, Eric Fisher—hence the name for my crypto, ErFi.

I fix my hair, spray myself with cologne, and put on my Rolex, all the while aware of Natalie tied and locked in the closet. She should have been a red flag from the start. I was hoping to tap that ass at the first opportunity. She's my type, despite being a little thick in the thighs. Not only did she not put out, but she was rubbing shoulders with the house manager.

Don't get me wrong, I like Julien. He's hardworking, dedicated, quiet, with an impressive résumé. And he knows how to kiss ass—brownie points. Let's hope Natalie didn't run her mouth and spill anything to Julien or the other staff about what she found out from Rich. Otherwise, I swear, the whole house will be a giant murder scene, and that's too much work for my liking.

I pick up the keys and pause, listening for any sounds from the closet. There's nothing. Natalie's out. When I get back, we'll have a chat, and then she'll join the fate of the others who thought they were smarter than me.

Oh, right, the sedative!

I walk up to the chest of drawers and open the top one. There are two rows of syringe cartridges—red and blue. The red ones contain a regular sedative. The blue ones are loaded with a nerve agent that's only used by the military. In regular doses, it doesn't kill but turns a person into a vegetable, unless it interferes with other medications, triggers an allergic reaction, affects a weak heart, or shuts down the kidneys—the list of side effects is a mile long. The average effect is severe enough—brain damage, loss of neurological functions, and amnesia. Nice and clean. I don't like things messy.

I pick up a blue cartridge and put it in my pocket. The meeting this afternoon is important. Coincidentally, it's probably the last time Phil will need to show his face, so the "blue pill" will come in handy.

61

NICK

I wait by the car for Phil to come out.

What's taking him so long?

Annoyed, I check my watch. My work phone beeps. I have two. One is my "Nick-The-Driver" phone. The other one is Geoffrey Rosenberg's official number. I can't trust Phil with handling any type of business conversations. Not even a text. His burner phone is merely for our communications and for his occasional adventures that I monitor closely. At meetings, he leaves his phone in the car. I'm always by his side. If anyone needs anything, his default answer is, "Talk to my assistant. He'll handle it." It's given him a mysterious reputation.

The door opens, and Phil, dressed to a tee, finally walks out of the house. But his sunken face is the opposite of what I need him to project today.

I nod and open the back seat door for him. He doesn't deserve riding in a Maybach, having a driver, or being treated like this. But, hey, the show must go on.

I close the door behind him and get in the driver's seat. Impatiently, I drive toward the gate, and as soon as we are out on the road, I let my anger out.

"That little housekeeper knows about you," I say, sucking my teeth in annoyance. "How?"

In the rearview mirror, I see Phil hang his head. Two days ago, he was spitting out insults in his drunken delirium. Now, his tail is between his legs. This guy is a classic addict.

He doesn't answer. Of course he doesn't. Clueless, as always.

"Well, she's dust," I say. "Because of you."

His eyes, sad and pathetic, meet mine in the rearview mirror. "What do you mean, *dust*?"

I swear, if I could kill with my stare, he'd be dead in a second. "I mean what I mean. Just like the other ones who got a whiff of your past. She'll have to disappear."

I brake at the red light intentionally hard, making him almost bash his face into the front seat.

Right away, his alarmed eyes meet mine in the rearview mirror. "Jesus Christ! How many more—"

My anger spikes tenfold, making me see red. Before he finishes, I reach back, grab him by the flaps of his suit jacket, and yank him toward me, making his stupid forehead bang on the front seat.

I let go and fix my suit jacket. "So goddamn irresponsible," I grit out and gun the engine on green.

"I didn't say anything!" he shouts, leaning forward, the tiny drops of his spit hitting my cheek.

"Oh, you *shout* at me now?"

I would've punched him, but visible bruises are bad for businesses. So I reach back again and punch his chest with the back of my fist. A weak punch, but it hurts. Oh, yeah, baby, it hurts.

Phil yelps in pain, holding his chest. He leans back and scoots to the farthest corner of the back seat, where I can't reach him.

"You never learn, do you? *Geo,*" I add bitterly.

"I'll text the house manager and tell him to fire her," Phil says, opening his phone.

There it is—stupidity in its rawest form.

I brake hard. Phil surges forward, and I reach back, yank the phone out of his hand, and slam it on the dashboard, then toss it onto the floor of the passenger seat.

"So tired of your shit," I grunt and take a deep breath, trying to calm myself but then remembering that I saw an unfamiliar number on his call log yesterday. That pisses me off again.

"Who's the chick you've been talking to?" I ask, trying to stay calm. "I have the number in your call logs. I can trace it to the name. Just tell me we don't have another problem."

"Mariah."

"Mariah what?"

"Mariah Dove."

"Mariah Dove, huh? Another fuck-toy? Does Mariah know that you are a fraud?"

"N–no."

"What does she call you?"

"Geo."

"And does Mariah invest in crypto?"

He sighs quietly.

I laugh in disbelief. "You kidding me? You are giving her insider information?"

Christ, he doesn't learn. That's why I need to get rid of him ASAP. This is the fifth skirt he's been feeding currency exchange intel. Maybe sixth—I lost count. Insider trading is illegal, but I know his argument—he's helping out because at the end of the day, this game has an expiration.

I turn up house music on the speaker. Music distracts me. Phil hates it. Perfect.

The Palisades Parkway is a steady drive, which is unusual for this time of the day. That's the only thing that levels my mood. For the next half hour, I try to calm down, despite the New Jerseyans' and New Yorkers' shitty driving. When I get to FDR Drive, the traffic thickens, but the driving takes my mind off the liability in my back seat.

Really, I can't play a tutor any longer.

If anyone deserves an acting award, that's me for playing a lackey for a year. And women in Manhattan should receive an award for being the number one gold diggers in the world, right along with those in LA. I can be the smartest, most handsome guy in a room full of rich old ugly assholes, and women will never pick me. Because, yeah, a driver.

Take Natalie. The second she heard I'm a driver, disappointment crossed her face. She hid it well. Must be professional. If I were Rosenberg, she would have put out the moment I offered her a job.

Bitch.

Maybe I'll fuck her before I pump her with drugs and send her to Neverland.

As I take the Broad Street exit into Manhattan's Financial District, I turn down the music.

Phil is quiet, sulking. That needs to change. I need him confident and at his best for the most important meeting of this endeavor.

"Listen, I didn't mean to snap," I say with as much reluctant politeness as I can muster. "It's…" I pause, deciding on the best word to use, and sigh with feigned remorse. "*Stress*, you know. We've been doing this for over a year." I cringe at the word *we* but continue. "One mistake, and it all goes out the window. One more meeting, and we are rich. What we are doing is more important than other people, right? We deserve this."

Phil's cowardly eyes shift to meet mine in the mirror, and I flash him a smile. Not overly cheerful but apologetic. He needs hope, at least for the next three or four hours.

"You'd never be able to make so much on your own," I say. "And I'd never be able to do this without you." Bullshit, but this pep talk has to work its magic. "We are going to be rich, okay?" I assure him. "So rich that you will have ten Mariahs hanging on your arms. Sipping cocktails in Rio. Riding a yacht in Morocco. We're almost there. You know that, right? I'm freaking out right now." I'm not, but that's irrelevant—I need to relate to this guy. "I'm on edge, and honestly, I'm shaking. I'm petrified. But this is all we've worked for."

Phil's gaze softens. "Yeah, I know."

To be fair, he didn't do any work, but just like a punished pet, he needs reassurance from the master. It's the carrot after a whip.

"I'm sorry for snapping," I say. "The tension gets to me. But we can do it, Phil. You and I." I look into the mirror and meet his gaze. I hold it, nodding, as I connect with his inner power animal. His is a raccoon, or maybe a worm, but it is what it is. "We'll be mega wealthy."

I reach behind my seat and offer him my fist for a fist bump. He obliges. He's used to my outbursts. And he desperately wants that promised piece of the cake.

I pull my Maybach to the curb in front of the financial building, which should already be swarming with investors waiting for us. Soon, we will make history. That will make me a billionaire while leaving thousands of others bankrupt in a matter of days. *C'est la vie.* Humanity never learns from its mistakes of trying to get rich on questionable promises by doing nothing for it.

Parked, I unbuckle, lean back between the front seats, and fix Rosenberg's hair. "Good. We are good." I inspect his face and suit. He's like a child, seriously, a grown man with peanuts for balls, but he does look GQ, and he carries himself well. That is, when sober and with proper guidance. "Are you ready, Mr. Rosenberg?" I ask in my most respectful voice.

He nods.

I nod back. "We are going to make history, yes?"

He snorts, but his smile is getting more confident. "Yes."

"I didn't hear you!"

"Yes!" he says louder.

I grab him by the back of his neck and bring his forehead to mine. "I didn't hear you, you rich bastard!" I shout with a smile.

"Yeeeeees!" he shouts back with a grin.

"Are we going to be filthy rich?" I roar.

"Yeeeeeees!" Phil roars back, shaking with anticipation.

And the show is on, ladies and gentlemen!

Thank god for the soundproof glass and tinted windows in my car.

The valet is already waiting by the curb. I jump out of the car, unhook my key chain, toss the rest of the keys at him, and open the passenger door.

"Mr. Rosenberg," I say with an important face, holding the door for Phil. When he gets out, I whisper, "Let's take this world by storm."

The fool is already puffing out his chest, his practiced

cocky face on as he confidently buttons up his ten-thousand-dollar suit, fixes his cuff links, and raises his chin.

Damn, occasionally I do like his third-rate acting. But it's the last time I'm opening the car door for this worm.

62

NATALIE

I wake up groggy and in the dark. It takes me a moment to remember where I am—that's still unknown, but I know who put me here—Nick.

I hear footsteps. Someone is here, though not in the dark space I'm in—a chest or a cellar—but on the other side of the door.

I'm afraid to make a sound. If it's Nick, this means he's back, and this time, I'm done for.

But when the door opens, unfamiliar boots step into my vision—work boots, or military, I'm not sure. I've never seen Nick wear those.

I squint, forcing my eyes up-up-up the black pants with a tactical belt and a black long-sleeved shirt. The silhouette against the light in the doorway is still blurry, and I can't see the face of the man who moves and drops to his haunches in front of me.

"I'm going to take out your gag and remove the ties, but you can't be loud," the low voice says, slightly familiar, though I can't place it. "Nod if you understand."

I nod.

He carefully pulls the gag out of my mouth. Then his gloved hand holds mine as he cuts the zip tie that's slicing into my wrists.

His gloves are rubbery to the touch, silicone maybe. It doesn't make sense. Who wears those? Why? What is this supposed to be—another kidnapping? Someone Nick sent? Are they going to kill me?

Thoughts change from one to another as the man removes the ties from my ankles and helps me to my feet. He holds me by the shoulders, steadying me, and I wince from pain in every joint of my body.

How long have I been lying on the floor unconscious?

"I'm not going to hurt you," he reassures me, not quite friendly, but not threatening either. "Everything is going to be fine. You are all right. Understood?"

I nod.

"I'm going to let go of you. When I do, you will not run, scream, or do anything stupid. Unless you want to get both of us in trouble."

I nod again, trying to collect the strength in my body.

Everything swims before me, slowly fading in and out of focus. My tongue is thick, my mouth dry. When the man lets me go and steps out of the dark space into the lit-up room, I realize that I was in the closet.

I blink repeatedly to bring things into focus and finally discern his face—it's Walter, the gardener.

63

NATALIE

Yeah, Walter is not a gardener—that's pretty clear.

"Did he hurt you? Besides the sedative he gave you?" Walter asks as he helps me to the couch.

"Define *hurt*," I say.

The room is fairly big and looks like a rental—no personal belongings, no framed pictures, no clothes, and standard furniture. The shutters on the windows are tightly closed, but the room is brightly lit.

Walter takes a seat at the computer desk, which features multiple monitors that resemble a professional IT setup. He fires up all of them at once and puts in the passwords.

That's not what surprises me though, and not the number of computers in this place, but why he knows the passwords. Is this his place?

A suitcase in the corner catches my eye, then the blue sneakers next to it. Nick's. This must be Nick's place! But if this is Nick's place, then I must be at the guest house. That means Nick might be somewhere around. This guy, Walter, has the key to this place, knows the passwords to the computers. He looks *at home* here.

I shift my feet to steady myself, even though I'm sitting, because a wave of nausea makes me dizzy.

Is Walter in on it with Nick? No, he can't be. Nick sedated me. Walter just took off my restraints.

I rub my wrists, which hurt from the zip tie. I swear, if I see Nick again, I'm going to knock him out with… I don't know. An axe? A baseball bat? I wish I had one. I scan the room, trying to figure out if I should find a weapon in case Walter tries something funny, too, though he seems uninterested in me.

A muffled beep cuts through the silence, and Walter presses his finger to the hem of his shirt, the push-to-talk mic clipped to it.

"She is okay, boss. Yes, she's fine…" He lifts his eyes to me while he listens to someone on his earpiece. "Okay… Yes…"

"What's going on?" I mumble, trying to get my tongue moving, though it still feels like a giant toad.

He ignores me. "Okay, boss. Got it… No, I didn't. She doesn't know… Okay. I'm getting them ready for you."

A chill goes through me. Who is the boss? If it's Rosenberg, I'm screwed.

"Who are you talking to?" I ask, dreading the answer.

Walter doesn't answer but starts typing away at the computer desk.

"How did you know I was here?"

"The tracking app on your phone," he replies without turning to look at me.

Of course, someone tapped into my phone! How could I be so stupid? Rich, the dead guy, warned me about it.

"What's happening?" I ask.

Walter doesn't answer.

"Hey! What's happening?" I repeat.

He throws a look at me over his shoulder. "You need to be quiet. I'm here to help, not to hurt you."

"Then tell me what's happening!"

"That's up to the boss."

"Boss who? Rosenberg? Nick?"

What if it's Nick? What if he changed his mind about getting rid of me? That's not exactly a reassurance. He is a freaking psycho.

"Why did Nick sedate me and tie me up? Where is he?"

"You need to stay quiet. You already almost ruined everything," Walter grits out without looking at me.

"I don't understand. What does Nick want from me?"

"He wants you gone. And that's the problem."

"It's not if you are here to get me out."

"It's not up to me. If it were, I wouldn't care. You jeopardized the entire operation."

"What operation?"

He doesn't answer.

"What operation?" I almost shout. "Who is in charge?"

That's when the front door opens, and a dark silhouette appears in the doorway.

My heart does a panicking thud, but a second later, I recognize the man stepping inside, and my jaw drops.

Julien.

I freaking *knew* something was up with him!

64

NATALIE

I'm trying to murder Julien with my stare while at the same time trying to pick my jaw off the floor.

This isn't the Julien I know. Gone is his formal suit. He's dressed in all black: tactical pants, long-sleeved shirt, army boots, and gloves. Gee!

He looks different, but it's not the unusual outfit that makes no sense. It's his expression. As he's walking toward me, my brain whispers, "Hey, spot five differences," and my jaw is still on the floor when Julien drops to his haunches in front of me.

The next thing blows my mind.

He shows his palms, his hands gloved—there's something strange about people wearing gloves around here.

"I'm going to check your vitals, okay?" he asks in what could pass for a bedroom voice if this were that kind of scenario.

"Is this your idea of flirting?" I ask without thinking.

The corners of his eyes crinkle, but the smile doesn't

break, and I suddenly realize what's so different about him—he's concerned about me. He's looking at me with care, and that—that!—is something Julien-Mister-Freaking-Warden has never done before.

"Natalie, I'm going to touch you, okay?" he repeats.

I nod. My head spins for a second, and I wonder if I should fake passing out, if he would give me mouth-to-mouth, if this cold-as-ice man is a decent kisser.

It must be the sedative still in my system. The thought is inappropriate and out of context. But when Julien reaches for my face and gently takes it between his palms, a pleasant shiver goes down my body.

Am I high? I am. Definitely.

"How are you feeling?" he asks.

"Dreaming, obviously," I say, not fighting him.

His expression softens even more. "Sense of humor is a good sign."

I lean into one of his palms, not on purpose, but because my head feels like it weighs twenty pounds, and his touch is comforting.

"Hold still," he prompts. "Look at me."

I release a sigh. He sounds like a gentle warrior, and I'd really like to cuddle right now and sleep.

Julien tips my chin with his fingers. "Natalie," he repeats softly, "look at me, please."

I do. His hazel eyes are so close that it feels almost intimate. His thumbs reach for my eyelids and gently pull them up, opening my eyes wider, inspecting my pupils. He's playing doctor, and I'm kind of liking it, though I'm not sure how he knows to check for signs of trauma.

"Is this your idea of foreplay or something?" I ask, my tongue still thick and heavy.

The corner of his mouth hitches in a tiny smile as he presses two fingers to the side of my neck to check my pulse, then lets go of me and stands up.

"She's good," he says, turning to Walter. "I'll take it from here."

Walter gets up from the desk too abruptly. "We don't have the passkeys," he says with slight hostility. "We can't wrap this up yet."

"We don't have time," Julien argues. "It's now or never."

"We have time! Leave her here, and we'll carry on in the way we were supposed to."

"You know what will happen to her then," Julien says firmly. "We can't."

"We are aborting this because of *her*?" Walter points a finger at me, his angry stare on Julien. "Are you *serious*?"

"I am," Julien says, his cold voice back. "There's been enough collateral damage. We can't keep doing this."

"Fuck!" Walter throws his head back.

"What's happening?" I ask weakly, rubbing my wrists.

Walter turns to Julien again. "We can make it look like she broke out of here and hide her elsewhere, get her off the property. We need time, man. We need to find the passkeys. We need to finish this. Otherwise, the entire year goes down the drain. It's not just about us. Thousands of people will suffer."

I close my eyes, trying to piece together bits of information.

"I know," Julien says sternly. "I will copy the files onto the hard drive, then get her out of here, and we will execute the emergency plan."

"How long?"

Julien pulls a phone out of his pocket and checks it.

"The tracker says they left Manhattan about ten minutes ago. They'll be here by ten. You do what you need to do."

Is it ten in the evening or morning?

Walter shakes his head, giving Julien a murderous stare, then storms out of the guest house.

Julien takes a seat at the computer desk, retrieves a hard drive out of his pocket, and plugs it into one of the computers. The screen immediately comes to life, showing rapidly scrolling lines of code, flashing text, windows opening and closing.

I have so many questions. Why is Julien here? How does Walter fit in? Why are they dressed like that? Why is he copying stuff off Nick's computers? Why does Nick have so many computers?

I silently watch Julien, waiting for him to explain, meanwhile observing his body language.

His elbows on the desk, Julien leans with his forehead onto his hands. He's either deep in thought or in some kind of trouble. After a short while, he shifts and picks up his phone again. I can't see what he's doing, but when I hear the familiar voices coming from it, they make the hairs on the back of my neck stand on end.

"The dinner with the board went well, right?"

It's Rosenberg's voice.

No one responds.

"What now? IxResearch is public. It's a done deal."

Silence.

"Nick, when do I get the money?"

Silence.

"I'm getting the money soon, right? Like you promised?"

Then comes Nick's voice.

"Shut the fuck up, okay? Let me think."

I gasp in shock.

Julien tilts his head to the side, as if it helps him hear better.

"Once we get to the house, this little circus is over," Nick says.

"What do you mean it's over? I need the money you promised."

"You will get what I give you. Everyone gets what they deserve."

"No one else will get hurt, right? We are going overseas, right? Under new identities. You said that." Rosenberg sounds hesitant, almost begging. *"None of those women deserved it."*

"Yeah, well, you should've kept your mouth shut."

"Nick! Let's just go, like you said—"

"Oh, now you feel sad? Now you feel sad, you piece of shit? How about—"

There's a loud thud, followed by a moan, and things go quiet.

Nothing about this makes sense. I gape at Julien, who presses the button on the mic clipped to his shirt. "Something else came up. I think Nick is going to get rid of Phil Crain… Yes, tonight. We can't let that happen. We don't finish this tonight, we lose him… We will try, yes."

"Julien, what's going on?" I ask.

"I will tell you later," he says dismissively.

"No, not later. Tell me now. And tell me what I have to do with all of this?"

He turns to me slowly, his gaze sad. "Nothing, Natalie. Except that you might have just ruined thousands of lives."

65

NATALIE

"Okay-okay-okay. Back up, Julien." I stare at him in shock. "You have a tracker on Rosenberg and Nick. Why?"

"Because I'm tracking them."

I whimper in frustration. I want to ask about the hidden camera but hold my tongue for now. Nothing about this house makes sense anymore.

"You knew Rosenberg wasn't who he said he was?" I ask.

"Yes." Julien detaches the hard drive from one computer and hooks it up to another one.

"And you knew that I knew?"

"Yes."

"How?"

"Your phone, Natalie. There's not a single step you made in this house without me knowing. Including your phone calls and texts. I apologize for that, but it was necessary."

"*You* took the letter out of my purse?"

"Yes. If Nick found out, it would've been a disaster."

"Nick?"

Julien turns to face me. "Nick is the man behind IxResearch."

I gape at him. "Nick, the driver?"

"To put things simply, Nick is the brain of IxResearch. The man that you know as Rosenberg is just a face, an actor. And the real Rosenberg is dead."

That's a lot to process, but I still don't understand why Julien is doing this. "So why don't you go to the police? This is identity theft."

"It's not as simple as you think. We can't just hand Nick over to the police. There's not enough evidence to implicate Nick in the IxResearch scam. He's that smart."

"Wait. What do you mean IxResearch is a *scam*? It's the largest crypto exchange in the US."

"It is. Nick took IxResearch, which was developed by the actual Geoffrey Rosenberg, and turned it into a billion-dollar company."

"And that's bad how?"

"It's not. Until Nick pulls the plug. He's slowly transferring funds to a number of offshore accounts. Today, the meeting in Manhattan made IxResearch shares public. Which means, as we speak, the company is flooded with investments, making its value increase like no other crypto company in history. If Nick gets anywhere close to Ix accounts, he will drain them. Even if Nick is arrested, he will never give up the passkeys. He will be rich, even in jail. And millions of people will lose money overnight."

My eyes dart to the screens. "Is that what those are?" I nod toward them. "His accounts?"

"Yes."

"But you can't access them?"

"No."

"So what are you doing?"

"Copying the info to the external drive in case we can find the passkeys."

"Where are the passkeys?"

"They are probably on some sort of thumb drive. We haven't found it yet. We spent months around him. Months searching everything, bugging his phone, his place, listening to every word he says. Nothing."

Nick's words ring in my ears. *My little feisty dragon guarding the treasure.*

Those words might be nothing. Or they might mean that the thumb drive is here, in this guest house.

Julien presses his finger to his earbud, then turns to me. "I need to put you somewhere safe while we deal with this."

"What's happening?"

"You need to be out of sight."

"Whose sight?"

"Nick's. And mine, while I'm dealing with him."

"What does *dealing* mean?"

"Something you shouldn't be witnessing."

Despite the chill running down my spine, I want to know more. "I want to confront that asshole."

"You can't, Natalie. You either go with me, so I can take you somewhere safe, or…"

I cock my head at him, daring him.

He blinks slowly. "Or I'll have to tie you up to keep you out of trouble while we deal with the situation."

"Tie me up? Really, Julien?"

"I am not joking," he says sternly, though his tone is not threatening.

"I am not either. I'll bite your nose off," I warn. I don't have a chance against this guy, but a girl's gotta try.

Julien's chest shakes in a suppressed chuckle. Obviously, I've gotten better at getting under his skin.

"Please, Natalie," he asks, and I think this polite version of Julien is really cute. "Please," he repeats even softer.

"Okay," I agree. "Where do you want me?"

I won't listen. No way I'm going to sit in hiding while the asshole who sedated me might escape.

Julien just doesn't know it yet.

66

NICK

The board meeting was a piece of cake. All those rich peacocks have no idea that soon, their dreams will come crashing down on them.

Neither does Phil.

I need to get him into my guest house. Next, I will drug him—I can't leave witnesses. Definitely not the one who knows the entire logistics behind the IxResearch scam.

I'm ecstatic. The music in the car is blasting. Despite my going off at the fool earlier, he looks cheerful. For the first time, he's in the passenger seat next to me, instead of in the back seat like a king. And he still doesn't have a clue.

In ten minutes, he'll go night-night forever.

As we pull up to The Splendors, I want to sing at the top of my voice. I've already packed the essentials: Ix paperwork, fake documents, and that sort of stuff. A flight to Singapore leaves at six in the morning. I don't need to be in the US—I can finish my business elsewhere.

The Splendors' gate opens, and the security guy salutes

me. I wish I could kick all the staff in their faces. *Morons.* All of them have looked down on me in the last half a year like I was some third-rate employee. Like them.

Not even close, idiots.

I drive up to the entrance and contemplate walking in and having dinner, like the king of the mansion that I am. I'm done slumming it in the guest house. On second thought, I'm so sick of this place and the stupid faces around me that I decide against it. I'd better not ruin my appetite with the chores I still have to do.

First, Natalie. Then Phil.

No. Maybe Phil first. He is a parasite I need to get out of my way, then I'll have a chat with Natalie, maybe fuck her. I do need to blow off steam. Then I'll give her the last injection.

I park my Maybach and check my phone. IxResearch shares were released to the stock market hours ago, and they are already raking in record numbers. *Good.* I can wait until midnight and then start transferring more company funds out. I only need my passkeys and a laptop. I can do it from the airport.

"Go to the guest house," I order Phil, who's still waiting for me to open the door for him.

"Why?" he asks, confused.

"Because I said so," I say and get out of the car.

Julien is walking out of the main entrance of the mansion. This guy somehow thinks he is superior to the rest of the staff, when in fact, he is here to follow orders like everyone else.

And he's walking slowly, with his hands cupped in front of him, the usual empty stare of a robot on his face.

Except, I notice the change in his clothes. That's

odd—Julien is dressed in all black, some sort of maintenance guy getup. Everyone is getting out of hand in this place.

I'd love to rub Julien's nose in the dirt. But as I see Phil getting out of the car, I realize that, in the staff's eyes, Phil is still the Rosenberg who hired them.

This is beyond annoying.

"I told you multiple times not to use the main entrance. It's not for the employees," I tell Julien. I'm done being a nice guy around here. "Mr. Rosenberg wants all the staff in the kitchen." I need all these ants in one place, so they don't interrupt what I'm doing for the next two hours. "There are things—"

I don't finish, because Julien moves so fast that I don't understand what's happening until electricity shoots through me like I touched exposed wires. My body locks up and then starts jerking uncontrollably. Words clog my throat. I'm shaking but I can't move my own limbs.

Behind me, Phil starts yelling and fighting with someone, but I can't turn to him, can't ask for help, can't do anything, paralyzed by the electric current. My eyes burn. My muscles twitch. My legs give out, and I collapse onto the ground.

67

NICK

I try to protest when Julien duct-tapes my hands and then wraps the duct tape around my body, pinning my arms to my sides. But I can't move, paralyzed by the zapper that the fucker used on me.

He slaps duct tape over my mouth, then hauls me to my feet.

"Walk," he orders, pushing me and holding me by the neck, his fingers digging into my flesh so hard that I wince and howl. But the sound that comes out of my mouth is a muffled moan.

Panting through my nose, I stumble forward.

Where's Phil? I can't turn to see what's happening, though I hear several pairs of footsteps behind me. If he gave me up, I'll kill the asshole. Especially this one, Julien. I should've known something was up with him—he always seemed too stiff for a house manager.

And it looks like he's leading me to my place, the guest house.

Fuck!

Natalie is there, in the closet, bound and gagged. Hopefully, she's quiet enough. If they find her, I'm in more trouble than I already am.

A sudden thought strikes me—she's in on this. She was hanging out with that scumbag blackmailer I got rid of. It dawns on me what they all want—probably the passkeys to the accounts. Maybe my crypto. They won't get it, no way.

My mind reels like an out-of-whack Energizer Bunny from the commercial. I can't have them poking around my computers.

I need to run. I can access my work from any computer. I just have to get away from here.

It's already dark outside, and I feverishly scan the garden in the back—this could be my escape. When we approach the guest house, I jerk out of Julien's grip and dart toward the garden.

Before I make it ten feet, a sudden, brutal force knocks me down. My face smashes into the ground, making me go blind with pain.

"Get up!" Julien barks. The weight on top of me lifts—he must've tackled me—and he jerks me to my feet.

I hear a subtle ding—my keys fall to the ground, but Julien doesn't notice, and I don't care right now. It's better this way.

"Move it." Julien's fingers dig into my neck again as he pushes me toward the open door of my guest house.

I sniffle, wincing in pain—I think I broke my nose. Anger blinds me. I swear, when I get out of here, I will find this guy and ruin his life, destroy every person dear to him, and turn his life into hell. Granted, this won't be the first time. There are plenty of worthless cockroaches in the world who don't deserve to breathe.

Inside the guest house, I see the gardener, who stands next to the couch like a bodyguard, dressed all in black like some sort of special ops guy. If this is the CIA, I'm screwed, but they still won't get what they came for.

On the couch, Phil sits like a saggy bag of potatoes, bound, gagged, his pathetic eyes on me. Maybe he isn't the rat after all. If these guys are government, Phil is the only one who'll come out of this lucky, considering that by now, he should've gotten a lethal dose of nerve agent.

Julien pushes me onto the couch, then walks to my work desk and starts up the computers. What I see next makes my blood boil—he's entering the passwords to get into them.

How? Argh! I want to punch him in the face.

He opens the spreadsheets of all my bank accounts, then walks up to me and rips the duct tape off my mouth. My skin burns like hell, making me scream in pain.

But glaring at Julien doesn't change his expression. There's no cruelty in it, no arrogance, no gloating. Like I said, a robot.

"Who are you working for?" I ask, licking my lips to soothe the burn and tasting blood trickling from my nose. "I'll pay you."

Julien sets his hands on his hips. "Where are the pass-keys?" he asks instead.

I turn to the gardener. "I'll pay you both."

The gardener stands with his arms crossed over his chest, the same indifferent expression on his face.

"We need the passkeys," Julien repeats. "I know they must be on a thumb drive."

Oh-ho-ho. Clever.

I smirk at him. "Who are you? FBI? CIA?"

"Passkeys, Nick. This will all go quicker and be less painful if you don't play hard to get."

"I don't know what you are talking about. Ask Rosenberg."

"I would've, if you hadn't killed him and buried him in the backyard of a Vermont cabin."

Shit.

Phil next to me whimpers, his eyes widening at me in horror.

This is more serious than I thought. How does Julien know about the real Rosenberg? No one knows! It's impossible!

Julien takes a step closer. "I would've, if this guy, Phil Crain"—he tilts his head toward Phil—"actually knew anything about IxResearch. Or Metrix Technologies. Or ErFi coin. But he doesn't."

Double shit. How does he know about me and Phil and my previous scam that I ran years ago?

"So I'm asking *you*, Nick. Or should I call you Eric Fisher? Or Jordan Ruff?"

No one—*no one!*—can possibly know so much about me or my previous aliases.

My mind is spinning fast as I try to wiggle my arms, testing the restraints, but they are tight, making me completely immobile.

Julien could be with the CIA. But then, there'd already be others here. He wouldn't be interrogating me here. He wouldn't be alone, with a gardener by his side, or whoever this guy is. So it's just the two of them, then.

Julien's gaze is cold, as always—this is astounding. I thought he was just a meticulous Tin Man. Turns out, he has a different background. Military, if I were to guess.

The gardener walks to the door, picks up what looks like a folding bench propped against the wall, and takes it to the bathroom.

My eyes follow—what in the hell is that?

Julien fists the front of my shirt and jerks me off the couch, onto my feet.

"Let's go," he says, dragging me toward the bathroom.

"What are you doing?" I hiss, trying to protest as he pushes me into the bathroom.

The portable bench is unfolded and set up in the middle of the bathroom. It's almost full-body length, tilted to one side. I see a rope on the floor and a jug of water.

"Wh-what is that?" I ask as Julien forces me down onto the bench, into a lying position, face up.

"This could've gone easier," he says, staring down at me, pushing the sleeves of his black shirt up. The gardener picks up the rope and ties me to the bench, my head tilted down. "But since we really need those passkeys, we will get them out of you in a different way."

Julien retrieves a stopwatch out of his pocket and checks it. "We'll do twenty-second intervals," he says to the gardener. "Three breaths in between."

The hell?

The gardener picks up a cloth, which turns out to be my old T-shirt, and spreads it over my face, blacking out the view.

"Wait!" I shout against the fabric, realizing where this is going. Bench, cloth, water—this is waterboarding, an interrogation technique. It's torture. And they are about to use it on me.

"I hope you like water, Nick," Julien says. A click of the stopwatch follows. "Start."

I open my mouth to protest, but suddenly water starts pouring over my face, clogging my nose, eyes, and mouth, and cutting off my breathing.

263

68

NATALIE

I try the door of the library, but Julien locked it from the outside.

Great. Sure, Julien has a plan—whatever it is—but I can't just wait this out while the guy who tried to kill me and Cara might get away with it.

"Heeeey!" I yell.

Where's Rosalie? Where's the maintenance guy? Anyone? Rosenberg, for that matter?

It's dark outside, must be close to midnight now. I have to do something.

"Well, I swore I'd never do this again," I murmur, "but…"

Desperate times require desperate measures.

I pull a hairpin out of my hair and carefully stick it into the door lock, feeling for the pins inside the lock.

The downside of growing up in a small town in the middle of nowhere is boredom. The downside of boredom is doing a lot of stupid things that potentially can land you in jail. Don't ask me how many locks I picked as a teenager.

Among other things, much stupider, that I did with friends for fun or while intoxicated.

Several minutes later, the lock finally gives, and I slowly turn the door handle.

The mansion is ghostly silent. I tiptoe into the hallway then make my way into the staff kitchen, which is empty.

Where is everyone?

Adrenaline thumping in my veins, I step outside through the staff entrance and trot toward the guest house.

Razor-sharp lines of light outline the guest house windows. Julien and Nick must be there. I step around the corner and scan the entrance door and the patio, lit up by a porch light. There's no one outside.

Muffled sounds come from the inside, and I walk around the porch, on the grass, intending to go to the other side and peek into the other windows, hoping to see what's going on.

A crunch under my right foot stops me as a solid object I stepped on digs into the sole of my shoe. I bend down to see what it is and find a set of keys. Picking them up, I study the silly key chain that I recognize—Nick's. The little Empire State Building is cracked, the little peak broken off, the mangled pieces falling apart. I pull at them, exposing the metal core and what looks like something that is definitely not a key chain.

"Holy crap," I mouth, staring at it, then shove it into my pocket and turn my attention to the building.

I tiptoe to one of the windows, but the thin slices of light are not enough to see what's going on inside. Nick has done a great job securing his house. Or office. Now that I think about what Julien told me, my mind goes crazy with the thought that Nick has fooled the entire world with this IxResearch scam.

I tiptoe to the door and hold my breath, turning the handle.

The person I see inside is the last person I expected to run into.

Rosenberg sits on the couch, his mouth taped shut, his arms duct-taped together and tight against his body.

I stall at the sight.

Days ago, I thought he was a wealthy entrepreneur, a powerful man with a brilliant mind and dark secrets. But his pleading eyes and useless jerking as he sees me and nods at his restraints makes him look pathetic.

"Four, three, two, one," Julien's voice counts down from another room, drawing my attention to the slightly ajar bathroom door.

What I hear next is a low and nasty gurgling sound, like that of an animal. A loud spitting sound follows.

"You lousy dipshits!" Nick shouts angrily. "You think you can harass me? Think twice! Wanna do it again?" He coughs. "Go for it! You won't get shit out of me!"

"Next round," says Julien. "Go. Twenty. Nineteen. Eighteen," he starts counting, his voice drowned by the loud splash and dripping sounds.

My heart in my stomach, I tiptoe toward the bathroom and peek in. The sight makes my eyes go wide in shock.

69

NICK

I focus on the water flow drowning my nasal cavities. After several seconds, I open my mouth and spit out the water, then close it and refocus on the water flow.

This is waterboarding at its finest. But only someone with military background knows how to do it properly, like this—making sure the water goes into my sinuses, not the lungs. And these two are doing it with a timer—it's government protocol. I've read about this many times, did proper research, just like I did on the illegal nerve agent drug I buy off the dark web.

When Julien counts down to one, the cloth is lifted off my face. I spit the water out of my mouth as hard as I can, aiming for his face, then snort some of it out and force a laugh.

"Morons," I hiss. "What, your little trick doesn't work?"

I used to be a swimmer in high school, a damn good one. Could have been a state champion if it weren't for the chronic sinus infection that I had to have surgery for. I left swimming behind, but the surgery did wonders for my sinuses. In fact, professional swimmers go through special training, learning underwater breathing techniques. But of course these stupid idiots don't know that.

I laugh into Julien's face, then swish saliva and water in my mouth and spit at him.

"Moron," I growl. "Good luck trying."

I can see slight disappointment crossing his face. No, not that—he's puzzled. *Good.* I'm a fucking genius. I've dealt with worse in my life, way worse than two guys on a wanna-be-*Mission-Impossible* quest trying to get all I've worked so hard for since college.

"I need the passkeys," Julien says more intensely now, like a parrot on repeat.

Suck it! He's better at flying past my radar with his botched management company and probably a fake name.

I force another laugh into his face, though my eyes burn from water, and so do my sinuses. He'll pay for this, I promise.

The gardener makes a move toward me with the soaking wet fabrics, but Julien stops him.

"In different circumstances," he says, his tone not even slightly changed, "I could work on you slowly and with less physical damage. But I'm afraid we are running out of time. And you deserve the worst, Nick." He nods to the gardener. "Ready?"

The gardener grabs a black bundle on the side of the bathroom counter and unrolls it.

My sight is blurry from the water, and my head is dizzy, but I catch a glimpse of what's inside that cloth—a row of stainless-steel objects, including knives, scalpels, and pliers. The ceiling light playfully reflects off their dangerously sharp steel edges.

I can deal with water, sleep deprivation, and punches. But not knives, pliers, and god knows what these two psychos are capable of.

My bladder goes weak, and I clench my jaw, hoping that I survive this, though I know already that these will be the worst minutes of my life.

But the gardener takes out matches.

"What's that?" I choke out.

"This," the gardener says, "is a match." *No shit.* He holds one in the air. "It will be inserted into your most private and sensitive organ."

His eyes drop to my crotch, and sudden panic slams into me.

"Then, I will light the match," he continues with sadistic satisfaction, making my breath catch in my throat at the terrifying visual. "And watch it burn as you scream in agony."

An angry smirk curls his lips as my entire body goes weak with terror. Before I can stop it, my bladder gives way.

70

NICK

"You can't do that," a soft voice says.

Both Julien's and the gardener's heads snap in the direction of the door.

"Natalie," Julien breathes, and for the first time, his steel expression falls.

The sinister match in the gardener's fingers stills. That match will be my undoing, I swear.

"I told you to wait it out in the library," Julien says, walking out of the bathroom.

First, how did Natalie get out of the closet?

Most importantly, why isn't Julien surprised to see her? Which means she somehow got away, or he freed her.

I freaking knew the guy had a thing for her. He's been breathing down her neck since I got her a job.

She just saw what happened, what *is* currently happening—my pants getting soaked by my own urine. I want to howl in anger and embarrassment. I will blow up this place and every single one of these pricks.

But right now, I lie very still, hoping that the match threat never comes to fruition.

"You can't do that," Natalie says behind the door.

"You weren't supposed to be here," Julien argues, "for the very reason that you don't understand what it takes to extract information from a person."

"Well, not what you were about to do."

"He is not a good guy, Natalie."

"No shit, Julien! But he doesn't deserve to be tortured!"

The little bitch actually sticks up for me—good.

"Did you get any information out of him?" she asks angrily.

Damn! That fire! I might've underestimated her.

"No. But I need you to step away, Natalie—"

"How about this?"

I can't see what she's doing, but the sudden silence is suspicious.

"Damn…" I think that's the gardener, his face turned toward the open door, his eyes widening.

"Where did you get this?" Julien asks.

"I found them outside the door, on the ground. It's a stupid Empire State Building key chain Nick carried on him."

Nooooooo!

Fury and frustration clash in me with such force that I start tugging at the stubborn duct tape, trying to break free. Failing. Failing-failing-failing. Argh! They can't have that! Not the passkeys! *That* bitch—I should've killed her when I brought her here. I've never hated a woman more.

"Bring Rosenberg to the bathroom," Julien orders. "Natalie, take a seat on the couch. I need to check this thumb drive."

An angry struggle follows. Phil is shoved into the

bathroom, and the door slams behind him, leaving him staring at me. He looks like a spooked rabbit that I'd love to club to death.

A moment later, the gardener returns. He undoes the ropes that tie me to the bench, then yanks me up and drags me into the room and toward the desk.

One of the computer screens is lit up with a message, Fingerprint authentication required.

"Be still," the gardener barks as he holds me from behind. Julien grabs my hand, yanking it closer to the computer, and presses my forefinger to the tiny panel on the thumb drive.

Thank you. Your access is authenticated, the sign flashes on the screen, and multiple windows open to reveal all of my offshore accounts with direct access to them.

The gardener drags me back to the bathroom, dumps me on the floor, and slams the door shut.

That's it. I'm screwed.

Angry tears burn my eyes. Seething with hate, I curl into myself, wanting to spill someone's blood right now.

I know what's going to happen next. Those guys will go through my offshore bank accounts, siphon all the money out—I'm sure they are thieves. If they are smart enough, they will transfer funds from IxResearch too—that's billions by now. And—

I want to roar, but I grit my teeth, then start banging my head against the floor, wanting to bash someone else's skull into pieces.

Almost everything I've worked for is in the hands of these thugs.

Phil whimpers behind me, then nudges me with his foot.

"What?" I snap at him in a whisper.

He widens his eyes and motions to his hands.

"Yes, they are tied, just like mine. Now what?"

Wiggling, I manage to sit up on the floor, thinking about what to do next. Kick those two when they come to get us? No chance. Make a run for it? Not a chance either. If they have anything to do with the government, more people will be here in no time, though I have a feeling these guys work on their own. That means that they want the money. Which means they won't call the cops.

Think, think, think, Eric!

Rosenberg steps closer and shoves his hands and torso into my face.

"What the hell?" I glare at him, bending back, trying to get away from his crotch.

His mouth is still taped up, so he can't talk. But he frantically motions with his eyes to his hands, then to my mouth, shakes his head like a naughty puppy, then shoves his duct-taped hands in my face again.

What does he—

Then it dawns on me—my mouth is not taped, so I can try to rip the duct tape off his hands with my teeth.

Brilliant!

Duct tape is unbreakable when you tug at it, but if you make a small cut at the edge and apply pressure, it rips like paper. So I do just that—bare my teeth and grind at the edges of the duct tape around Phil's wrists. In seconds, his hands come loose.

He rips the duct tape off his mouth, silently screaming and cursing under his breath, then rips the rest of the duct tape off his body.

"Get this off me," I order in a whisper, wiggling on the floor until I finally get to my feet.

Phil flinches, shaking his head.

"Phil," I hiss, nudging my hands at him. "Help me out."

His sheepish stare doesn't change.

Oh, crap. The guy is flaking out on me? Now, of all times?

He shakes his head again and takes a step away from me.

Well, crap. I really did a number on him. Should've been nicer, but he deserved it. Except now, he says the last thing I want to hear.

"You killed the real Rosenberg?"

71

NICK

Even the smartest sheep willingly go to a slaughterhouse if given an incentive.

"Phil," I whisper. "We need to get our money. We need to get out of here, find a safe place, and get the money back."

He breathes heavily, his stare on me both doubtful and hopeful at the same time.

"Come on, man," I plead. I can't believe I'm begging this idiot. "This is our only chance. This or prison. For life."

"I did what you told me to do. It's all you."

"Nah, man. Your face is everywhere. Your signature is on all the legal documents. But I won't let them put you in prison. We need to get out of here and out of the country. I have plenty of funds." I nod toward the living room. "They can keep their stupid money. I have more. Much more."

In seconds, Phil rips the duct tape off my hands and torso.

See? That's the power of money-talk.

I exhale in relief, rubbing my stiff wrists.

My head is buzzing from all the water I swallowed.

My pants are wet from pee—just freaking great. I listen to the sounds from the living room, the hushed conversation between Julien and the gardener. I'm sure they are fascinated with the numbers they see in my bank accounts—it's all right, I'll take my revenge later.

My eyes go to the bathroom window. It's a large two-panel window covered by blinds. And that'll be our escape.

"What now?" Phil asks, nervously rubbing his hair with both hands. He finally looks like the worthless gambler that he is, but I need him. Window, backyard, garden fence that goes into the utility road behind it—I need Phil to give me a lift to get over that fence. Then I'll leave him behind.

I push him out of the way, carefully lift the blinds while making as little noise as possible, and open one of the window panels.

"Come on." I motion to him. "Be very quiet."

Thank god for the one-story guest house. The windowsill is only three feet off the ground, which I cross in seconds. This side of the guest house is hidden by shadows, which is great.

Phil pants and crouches like a raccoon as he clumsily jumps off the windowsill as if it's the third floor.

"Follow me and stay close," I order. "We need to hurry."

I trot along the side of the guest house, toward the back, and then dart as fast as I can across the lawn to the back garden. It's close to a football-field length, but as long as I can make it to the other side of the property's fence, I can hide out in the bushes while they search for me.

Wind whistles in my ears as I run. My heart races. I don't look back to check if Phil is following—he'd better be.

I trip over something on the ground, stumble, fall, and roll like a sack of potatoes.

"Christ!" I howl, feeling pain in every limb.

"You all right?" Phil is by my side, panting, too, as he bends down, hands on his knees, staring at me.

It's dark here. The only dim light comes from the sparse solar garden lights sticking out of the ground. My white button-up is soaked with water and sweat, and so are my pants. I get up and hiss, feeling the burn in my right ankle.

"Help me," I tell Phil. "I think I sprained my ankle. We should be only a hundred or so feet from the back fence."

I've never actually seen it, except in the property pictures I looked at before renting this mansion.

Loud voices in the distance make my nerves shoot on edge. "Quick. They're on us!"

A radio beeps from that direction, and that's all it takes for Phil to swing his arm under mine, holding me around the back, and help me move forward. He's taller than me but has never done any exercise. Nevertheless, it must be adrenaline, or the promise of money, or the threat of prison that makes him move fast, hauling me forward with astonishing strength as I limp along.

I see a light ahead. They must have lights along the property line. As we hurry among the trees and shrubs, the pathway clears, revealing the fence.

Well, what do you know?

The eight-foot fence has an opening with a small waist-high metal gate with a lock. Dumb, really, considering that anyone can jump over it in seconds. It's the camera mounted on top of the fence, pointing at the gate, which makes me grunt in frustration.

I'm sure someone is watching us, but I can't worry about it right now, because the voices in the distance get closer.

I'll easily get over the gate myself. My thumb drive is

in the wrong hands—nothing I can do about it. But I have another little stash back at the guest house. I'll find a way to get it back, but there's no way I'm sharing it with Phil. I really don't have time for a pep talk with him either.

I push him away and fish in my pants pocket, finding what I'm looking for—the syringe cartridge. It's meant for Phil, who is kicking the gate lock, trying to break it but failing.

"We'll just have to crawl over it," he says, turning toward me when I pull the syringe out and, popping the cap off, lunge at him.

I'm fast. I'm super fast. Usually. But this time, only a split second before I reach Phil, aiming for his neck, my ankle gives out with a sharp, awful pain that makes my legs weak. I howl and collapse against the gate just as Phil jumps away.

"What are you doing?" Phil cries out.

He watches me from a safe distance, wide-eyed like an owl, as I scramble to my feet.

Realization dawns on him. "You! Liar!" he shouts, his chest rising, his eyes darting to my hand that holds the syringe. He knows what those are—he's seen me use them, though most of the time, when I had to sedate the girls, he was drunk.

I can't argue, but I need to pull off a lie one more time. Phil can't stay alive, absolutely not.

"I need this injection," I lie, hoping that he falls for it again. "It's a painkiller. Otherwise, I won't make it."

My ankle hurts like a mother, but I clench my teeth and hoist myself up. My back is purposefully turned toward Phil. I need to fake more pain and confusion to get close to him.

"Give me a second, buddy," I pant, pretending to roll up my sleeve for an injection, meanwhile swaying, hunching, stumbling backward toward him.

When I sense him closer, I swing around, throwing all my weight at him.

In the blink of an eye, he grabs both my hands and rams into me, slamming me against the fence.

"You scumbag!" he yells and throws a punch into my face.

The pain is so sudden and sharp that I see stars.

"You liar!" he roars, punching me again.

"Traitor!" he snaps. A kick in my gut folds me in two and cuts off my breathing as my entire body stiffens in unimaginable pain.

"I lied for you! Cheated! Gave up my career!" he sobs.

I want to tell him that he was scum and a loser when I met him, but I can't talk, can't even take a breath. My eyes are shut as I try to work through the pain.

"There! Get them!" someone shouts in the distance, but closer, much closer, too close for my liking.

"You wanted a painkiller?" Phil asks in a threatening voice I know only from when he's drunk.

My eyes snap open and search for the syringe on the ground—I must've dropped it when this asshole hit me.

"I'll give you a painkiller," Phil growls.

My eyes dart to his hand, raised in the air, the familiar syringe now pointing at me.

"No," I gasp. "No-no-no-no-no." I back up, limping. I can't have what's in that capsule. "Phil, listen to me."

But before I come up with a good ploy, he lunges at me, and I squeal from the sharp pain of the needle in my neck.

I want to protest, but it's too late. Horror paralyzes me. I try to think of the antidote, though there's none besides an immediate IV. My body suddenly feels numb, making me sag against the fence and onto the ground. My chest tightens, making it hard to breathe.

Two figures come running—Julien and the gardener.

The gardener tackles Phil while Julien stands over me, his head cocked in amusement.

"What's wrong with him?" he asks.

"His painkiller," Phil says, panting against the grass as the gardener straddles him, tying him up.

"Painkiller, huh?"

I have a feeling Julien knows that it's not.

"It's not," I try to say, but my words sound like a senseless rasp.

I don't know what Julien has against me, but he's the only one who's ever figured me out.

I try to move, but I know how this works—my body is slowly going into paralysis.

"You finally got a taste of your own medicine," Julien says with a smirk, his features blurry.

You asshole is my final thought before the world goes dark.

72

NATALIE

They walk out of the dark garden like a team of survivors.

Walter, pushing Rosenberg in front of him, who's bound again, his mouth taped.

Julien, with Nick's body thrown across his shoulder.

I stare in awe at how strong Julien is, how different he looks in army boots and tactical pants. Their group shadow, cast by the porch light of the guest house, is dark and gigantic.

I step aside, letting them into the guest house.

This time, Walter sets Rosenberg down in a chair. Julien dumps Nick's body on the couch.

"What's wrong with him?" I ask, staring at Nick, who is motionless.

"I guess his buddy injected him with his own medicine," Julien says indifferently.

Goose bumps cover my skin. I shouldn't feel bad. After all, Nick was the one poisoning the girls all this time. He killed at least one person. I would've been dead, too, if it weren't for Julien.

Yet, the thought that he's poisoned gives me whiplash.

"We should take him to the hospital," I say, turning to Julien, who's already at the desk, doing something on the computer screens. "What are you doing?"

"Erasing the passkey security protocol so that the authorities can gain access to the system."

"What authorities?"

"The ones who will properly handle IxResearch funds and investments."

"You work for the authorities?"

"No."

"Then why?"

Walter leaves Rosenberg and walks up to me. "You ask too many questions." He turns to Julien. "I told you she'd be a liability."

I want to snap back with a clever remark, but I don't know what their plan is and how I fit in.

"Leave her alone. I'll deal with her," Julien says. "I've got all the accounts sorted, except for one, his personal money. We are keeping it," he tells Walter. "The rest will cover everyone, going back to Metrix Technologies."

"Good. Let's go. We need to hurry."

Julien gets up, leaving the computer screens on. "Come with me," he says to me, motioning toward the door.

"Where?" I ask, uncertain if I should follow. "I'd rather wait for the police."

Walter snorts. "You kidding me?"

Julien holds the door open for me. "We are done here. You are never coming back here. And that's not a request."

"And them?" I nod toward Rosenberg and Nick.

"The ambulance will arrive in time. As well as the police. I'll explain on the way."

But something doesn't sit right with me. If Nick's biggest asset was the thumb drive with the passkeys, then what did his reference to the treasure in the closet mean?

"What was Nick talking about when he mentioned a treasure?" I ask.

Julien nods to the computer. "This. Natalie, please, we really need to go."

I shake my head. "No. Something else. When he left me in the closet, he said that I was a dragon guarding a treasure."

Julien's eyes narrow, then shift to Walter, who walks toward the back of the living room and opens the closet. He inspects it thoroughly, knocking on the walls, then stomping on the carpeted floor. Julien and I watch when he stomps on one particular spot several times, then whips a folding knife out of his pocket. He cuts into the carpeting, rips part of it open, then stabs into the wooden planks underneath, and one of them comes loose.

"Bingo," he murmurs and takes out a tin container. Inside it is a flat rectangular box.

"What is it?" I ask.

Walter walks up to us and passes it to Julien. "More evidence of his crimes? I hope it's something good."

Julien pockets it and nods to me. "We have to go, Natalie. Now."

The night is warm, but when we step outside, I shiver. My head spins with the thoughts of how this is all going to play out. I'm in trouble. I'll have to tell the police about Rich, and Cara, and Nick, and the girl from the party. Oh, what a mess! I hope that I didn't do anything illegal. Detective Dupin will be shocked.

I follow Julien to the staff entrance of the house while Walter walks behind us, his finger pressed to the earpiece in his ear. "Understood. Yes. We are out… Guest house is the only one, yes. Ambulance, fire trucks, and the police. Yes. Ten minutes… Start the clock." He calls for Julien. "Boss, it's ready."

We approach the staff door, but Julien nods toward the van with his company's logo on it.

"Get in," he orders.

"Ready for what?" I ask.

He rolls his eyes. "Natalie, get in. *Please*."

Reluctantly, I get in and fasten my seat belt, hoping I won't end up at a bus stop in the morning, unconscious and with little brain activity.

Julien gets into the driver's seat, turns on the engine, and pulls out of the parking lot. The entrance gate is open—that's strange. No one greets us, and the security booth is deserted—even stranger. But as we drive away from The Splendors, I finally feel relieved.

"Where are we going?" I ask.

"I'm taking you home, Natalie. You're fired."

I snap to look at Julien and notice a little smile on his lips. Julien is joking. Julien-the-freaking-Warden is joking!

I blurt out a laugh. Then another one. I start laughing, unable to stop, but in seconds, my laughter turns into sobs, and I hide my face in my palms, crying uncontrollably and unable to hide it.

I was so stupid. So, so, so stupid!

The exhaustion, the fear, the stress of the last five days finally bombard me with all their intensity, and I'm crying like a baby into my hands. I cry for Cara, who's still in the hospital, who never came out of this safely like I did. I cry for Darla, who didn't make it. For the real Rosenberg, who might've been a good person. For a number of other women who fell victim to a charismatic cunning man.

Suddenly, a distant explosion shakes the ground, making the van rattle for a second.

Alarmed, I look out the passenger window and cover my mouth in horror. "Oh my god."

The night sky is lit up as the large flash of a giant explosion spreads over the landscape.

"Julien, it's The Splendors!" I turn to look at him, way past caring that tears soak my face.

He seems unfazed, his eyes on the road, his expression back to the so-familiar indifference.

"Must be a gas leak," he says coldly.

"But the guest house!"

"The guest house and everything inside it is fine."

Shocked, I lean back in my seat, slowly turning my gaze to the highway in front of me.

The lit-up skyscrapers of Jersey and New York loom ahead like a myriad of star showers against the black sky. They are so alluring with promises of a bright future, though many fall into their trap and fail.

I wipe the tears on my cheeks with the back of my hand.

"Must be a gas leak," I repeat quietly.

73

NATALIE

Julien pulls the van over by the door to my apartment building. At this point, asking him how he knows where I live is silly.

I'm scared and exhausted, wondering if the police will come knocking on my door at any moment.

"What about Rosenberg and Nick?" I ask.

"They are probably getting arrested as we speak. The computers at the guest house have all the information a proper cyber team needs."

I nod.

"No one can know about what happened at the mansion," Julien says as he kills the engine. "Neither what happened, nor that you were there, nor that you even know Rosenberg or his driver or anything about them."

His words start a light tremor in my body. I know I'm involved in something big, something dangerous, and keeping quiet about it makes me petrified.

How am I supposed to do that? What will I tell Detective

Dupin? As soon as she finds out about the mansion fire and who the mansion belonged to, she'll be all over me.

Julien reaches under his seat, pulls out a thick envelope, and passes it to me. "That's twenty grand."

I stare at it in shock, then raise my eyes at him. "Wh-wh—"

"For your silence."

"That means you trust me?" I muse, accepting the envelope. "When do I see you again?"

"Never?"

My heart hitches in disappointment, and I don't hide it.

Julien notices. I realize he's always noticed everything. "I thought you'd be relieved to get rid of me."

"I need answers, Julien."

"I think you have all you need, Natalie."

"I don't."

"That's all you need to know right now."

"What if I go to the police?"

Surprisingly, he doesn't flinch. If this were Nick, I would've been dead just for saying this. Julien? Somehow, I know he trusts me. Somehow, he knows I won't say a word.

"You won't," he says calmly.

See?

"How do you know?" I say, matching his tone. I'm not trying to bait him. It's a simple inquiry, and he knows that, not an ounce of resentment on his face at my words.

"I'm going to tell you what happens if you do." His gaze shifts to the street, assessing the neighborhood. "Any paperwork the police discover will lead to Nick's previous aliases. There won't be any proof that other people were at The Splendors. Everything burned down. All evidence is gone. All security footage is gone. All the traces of the staff management company that worked for Rosenberg is gone. Everything has been destroyed."

"The gas leak."

"The gas leak, yes, among other things. In fact, there won't be any traces of you either. Rosenberg doesn't know your last name or anything about you. No one should be able to find you. I made sure of it. You were a complication and extra work, but it was all taken care of."

I can see why I annoyed him when I arrived at my new job.

He turns to face me. "So if you do go to the police, nothing you say about the other staff will have any credibility. But you know about Nick's accounts. I have a picture of you with him in the garden. Another one in his car. As well as you and the so-called Rosenberg in his room. He and you will be the only live witnesses who have any ties to IxResearch. So guess who will be watched by the FBI for the rest of eternity?"

I feel a pang of disappointment. "You set me up."

"No. But that's how it's going to play out if you go to the police. It's only going to work against you."

"I won't. I think you know that."

"I do. I'll make sure they never get a whiff of your connection to The Splendors. If they do, I'll figure out how to sort it out."

"What about the detective I called? I did talk to her, Julien."

"I'll take care of that, too."

I raise my brows at him.

He gives me a little nod. "I will. Don't answer unknown numbers in the next several weeks."

"I assume you'll keep tabs on me?"

He nods again, not breaking eye contact. His voice is unusually soft. This conversation feels almost intimate, as if we aren't discussing how to avoid law enforcement and conspiracy charges.

"How?" I ask. "How are you so good at this? What's your background? Military?"

"Something like that."

Not good enough. "Intelligence?"

"Something like that."

"You won't tell me, will you?"

This time, he doesn't answer.

I snort. "Even though the mansion and the structures burned down, they might find fingerprints. Yours are in the system, I assume."

"They won't."

"You seem very sure."

He turns his hands palms up and shows them to me. He rubs his fingertips together, and I notice a strange texture covering them.

"What is that?"

"Silicone pads."

"Fingerprint-proof?"

"Yes."

"Wait, how... Do you... You couldn't have possibly worn them every day for months."

He doesn't answer.

"Jesus Christ, you did, didn't you?"

No answer. That's military training all right.

"You need to leave town for some time," he says.

"I'm not sure I can. My friend Cara, she—"

"She regained consciousness."

I stare at him. "When?" My heart flutters.

"This afternoon."

"How do you know?"

No answer.

I roll my eyes. "Wow. Okay. It's… Yeah…" I couldn't possibly imagine the extent of his surveillance.

Julien shifts in his seat. "At some point, your friend will have questions, especially when the news about Rosenberg breaks. She'll probably talk about it. You can't tell her you know what happened. You can't tell her anything. I understand you two are close, don't ask how I know. But she can't know about your involvement."

"Why? Why Rosenberg? Why Nick? Don't tell me you did it because of some Robin Hood ideals to return the money to the people who were scammed and prevent the biggest crypto disaster?"

My phone rings. *Dupin* lights up on the screen, and I swallow hard, shifting my eyes to Julien.

"Answer," he says.

"Julien, this is—"

"Answer," he commands, without telling me what to say to the detective and how to act.

"Hello?" I say timidly when I pick up.

"Miss Olsen, you are not a good listener, are you?" Detective Dupin says.

My breath hitches in my throat—she must know I went back to The Splendors, despite her advice.

"I'd love to say that wasn't smart on your part," she continues, "but turns out, you are quite a lucky charm."

Huh?

"Pass the phone to the man next to you," the detective requests.

"Wh-what man?" Panicking, I turn to Julien.

"Miss Olsen? Please, pass the phone to Julien."

My mouth opens in shock.

"It's for you," I say, passing Julien the phone as he takes it with no surprise whatsoever.

"Yes," he says into the phone. "Yes. Good. It's all done, then?"

I gape at him as he nonchalantly checks the neighborhood.

"She's fine, yes… Yes, on the same page… Good, good…" There's an unusual satisfaction on his face. "I love you too," he says and hangs up.

The last words make the world around me spin on its axis. Thoughts are scrambling in my head. I can't find the right words. I can't even put together the events that took place in the last several days.

Julien looks almost apologetic when he meets my eyes.

"To answer your question why—I did it for her." He nods at my phone.

Confused, I absently take it from his hand. "You mean Detective Dupin?"

"She's not a detective. And her real name is not Lesley Dupin either."

A crazy laugh is about to escape me, though I'm not sure if I feel like laughing or throwing up from exhaustion and shock. Julien goes quiet, but this time this won't do. "Care to explain?"

"She is my sister. She was involved with Nick, a long time ago. Before Ix. Before Rosenberg. I was working overseas and never met him. Then he did something unforgivable."

I stare in shock. "Like the other girls?"

Julien's lips tighten, and his gaze hardens. "I'm not going to get into details, but he tried to get rid of her. She almost died in a car crash he was responsible for. Two months in ICU, seven reconstructive surgeries, damaged vocal cords, miscarriage, damaged motor functions, permanent limp—that's to name a few."

"Oh, god," I whisper.

"When I found out what happened—after my sister recovered—I decided he wasn't going to get away with what he put her through."

"And many others."

"Yes. He deserves worse than what he got."

"You are telling me that you tracked Nick years ago, kept an eye on him, and started years-long surveillance to avenge your sister?"

"You think that's crazy?"

I don't know what to think anymore, but I really want to get to know this man.

"That's crazy, yes. And admirable. And..." I drop my gaze, trying to find the right words. "I don't know you at all, but you might be an incredible man, Julien. The true Man of the Year. Can I see you again?"

There, I'm making a move on a guy. It's not the first time but definitely rare.

His eyes keep me hostage for some time.

"It's not a good idea," he says softly, and I can see regret in his eyes that resonates with the rejection I feel.

Embarrassment makes my cheeks hot, and I smile, biting my lip.

"That blond girl in the library, by the way—thank you for alerting me about her being spiked. She got help in time."

I nod. *Good.* So he did take care of her.

Julien gets out of the van, walks to the passenger side, and opens the door for me. I suppose I overstayed my welcome. I get out and stand in front of him, just like the first day we met when he told me I wasn't welcome. Somehow, this feels like a very sad goodbye, though he was insufferable just a few days ago.

"Well, it was nice knowing you," I say. "It actually was. Though I'm pretty sure I was a pain in your butt."

"You ended up helping us. Thank you. You have no idea."

I want to keep this conversation going just a little longer, but I know there's no point. "Is that it, then?"

He nods.

"Right." I nod, mimicking him. "I guess I should go."

Julien offers his hand for a shake, and I give him a feigned suspicious look. "Oh, *now* you want to shake my hand?"

But I do, and that gets a little smile out of him.

"Well, goodbye, Julien."

"Goodbye, Natalie," he says softly and lets go of my hand.

I start walking away. Just as I step to the front door of my apartment building, I hear Julien's voice. "Natalie?"

He's standing by the van's driver's side, watching me. "Change the lock on your apartment door. It sucks."

This man, seriously…

"And if I were you, I'd get a new phone and make it password-protected." He winks.

I don't respond, only put the tip of my fingers to the side of my forehead in a military salute.

For the first time, Julien grins at me. It's a beautiful grin that makes my heart break just a little bit.

74

NATALIE

I was sedated, kidnapped, almost died, and watched the biggest scam of the year go up in smoke, yet my priority is a rat.

"Sorry, Trixy," I murmur to our pet, who's been alone overnight.

She restlessly pounces at the cage bars as I refill her food bowl. I need to visit Cara at the hospital, but first, I need a nap, so I lie down on the couch and pass out for hours.

It's early afternoon when I wake up.

First things first, I stuff my mouth with a nutrient bar, starving but too exhausted to cook. Then I check the news.

Sure enough, The Splendors' fire is breaking news. So is IxResearch and Geoffrey Rosenberg. The fraudster's face is all over the front pages of all online newspapers and blogs. Except this time, it's a picture of him being led by the FBI in handcuffs, amid the burned-down ruins of The Splendors Mansion. The only standing structure is the guest house in the background. Rosenberg doesn't look very sad. Whatever he was promised by Nick is now gone, but so is Nick, and knowing what that guy was capable of, I think Rosenberg, or whatever his name is, is the luckiest guy alive.

Do I feel bad about hiding the truth of what went down? Well, those who say that truth is sacred are full of crap. Many things are more important than the truth. Justice, safety, and happiness—those are just a few that law enforcement can't always guarantee. Truth doesn't pay the bills. I'm coming to terms with the current situation alarmingly quickly. But a girl's gotta eat. And I have to take care of Cara.

Next on my agenda is to get my car from downtown by the coffee shop, buy Cara's favorite muffins and coffee, and drive to the hospital. Since she's awake, she might want some of her belongings, so I go to her room and pick up her iPad, a book on her nightstand, and a recent magazine that sits on top of a pile of costumes.

When I pick it up, I spot a familiar name on the cover— *Geoffrey Rosenberg.*

Oh, Cara…

I flip the magazine to the article about the Man of the Year, and stare at his picture.

One man is making waves in the crypto exchange world, and he is about to become the Crypto King.

Cara must've seen this too, recognized him in the club, and knew that he was loaded.

"He's my jackpot."

I'm about to put the magazine away—she doesn't need a reminder—when something falls out of it and lands on the floor.

It's a photograph, a group of people in the greenroom of

the Bleecker Theatre. I know that because I've been there, partying with Cara, Lindsey, and some of the actors seven years ago. The theater shut down when we were still in college.

In the picture, Cara's head is tilted back as she drinks right out of a bottle. Yep, that's Cara.

I smile as I study the others in the picture. And then my eyes pause on the person second to the right, a man with blond hair, blond eyebrows, and blue eyes. Though it's a different look and he's wearing some sort of costume, he's unmistakable—Geoffrey Rosenberg.

My breath hitches in my throat. "Holy moly, Cara," I whisper.

Next to him is another face I recognize. The floor falls under my feet—it's Rich, the stalker.

Girl, what did you get yourself into?

I turn the photograph over and read the writing.

Pat's Birthday. Pat, Cara, Jenny, Jim, Phil, Rich.

I count the people—yep, the man who's a spitting copy of Rosenberg next to Rich is named Phil, just like Rich said.

So Cara knew him and Rich, worked with them. Last week at the club, she knew that Rosenberg was an impostor. So did Rich. Did they plan on blackmailing Rosenberg together, or did they want the insider information for the crypto exchange?

"He is my jackpot."

Rosenberg was neither a jackpot nor the Man of the Year. He was a pawn, and I'm glad Cara survived him and Nick.

On second thought, I'm lucky that I did too.

I pack a bag to take to the hospital. I still don't know

what Cara's condition is. If she has partial amnesia, I hope she forgets ever running into Rosenberg, a.k.a. Phil, and Nick.

If her brain has more damage than that, we will get through that too. We will. We can. We are small-town girls in a big world, and we've learned to crawl through the mud. Because where we come from, the roads are narrow, mud is everywhere, and we learned to appreciate new opportunities. We also learned to deal with Rosenbergs and Nicks. Nick being gone is not exactly revenge, but it's closure.

Closure is not always justice.

Sometimes, closure is knowing that other people won't get hurt in the future, and that's a big thing.

EPILOGUE

NATALIE

A YEAR LATER

SANTORINI ISLAND, GREECE

"Take your time!" Cara yells from the private spa room, which is larger than our Jersey City apartment.

That's the thing you find out while staying at an island resort—not every room that has a toilet and a shower is called a bathroom. The one in our villa has a bathtub, a steam shower, and a mini salt room, and is called "a private spa room."

Currently, Cara is lying in a stone bathtub filled with warm water and bubbles. An arched window overlooks the caldera. Santorini Island is gorgeous, and Cara says that we should move here. Despite my online freelance jobs that give me freedom to work from anywhere, I don't think we can afford to live in Greece yet, though it's definitely on my bucket list.

"I'm getting pastries and coming right back!" I shout back.

I lock the door and take the narrow stone path between the whitewashed buildings to the local bakery.

It's early morning, and the street is deserted. Ocean waves crash against the shore in the distance. Salty breeze, amazing local food—the several days we've spent on the island so far have been nothing short of amazing.

While I don't talk to Cara about what happened a year ago, it's always on my mind. I hate lying. Technically, I *am* going to the bakery for fresh pastries. But I'm more curious about the latest *Time* magazine article about IxResearch. So when I get to the bakery, I briefly chat with Christina, the owner, all the while eyeing the *Time* magazine lying on the side of the counter and eventually pick it up.

A familiar face stares back at me from the cover.

Well, hello.

The headshot is split in half. Half of it is red-haired Rosenberg, with a cocked brow, confident and cold, with a green eye. The other half is Phil Crain with outgrown blond hair, stubbled chin, saggy eyelid, and blue eye.

ONCE MAN OF THE YEAR.

NOW AN EX-CONVICT.

WHAT DOES THE FUTURE HOLD FOR ONE OF THE BIGGEST FRAUDS OF THE CENTURY?

Phil Crain is fresh out of prison. He got off easy. Apparently, he is a victim in this story. It's a universal truth that assholes live forever.

The sight of him yanks me back to the days at The Splendors Mansion a year ago, the days that still feel surreal, something I dreamed up.

For weeks after The Splendors fire, the story was all over the news. I didn't leave home, waiting for someone—anyone—to knock on my door. But there were no unexpected visits from the police or FBI, just like Julien had promised.

I read everything I found online about the case. Nick ended up in a coma, in the hospital, and died several days later from complications from the chemical he was injected with.

A week later, Cara was released from the hospital with minimal brain damage except for dizziness and memory issues. I took her on a road trip to New Hampshire, where we stayed at a secluded rental cabin for several weeks. Cara told me about Phil Crain and her dealings with Rich. I pretended to be angry about her never letting me in on the story. But I couldn't be angry when I was hiding so much more from her.

During those weeks, I scanned the news and crypto blogs daily. There were so many theories about what had really gone down at The Splendors, but none of the bloggers or investigators got the story right. They suspected the Freemasons, the BlackRock corporation, the World Economic Forum. Some proposed Russian KGB involvement, because one of the names mentioned by the reporters was Russian. Probably "Natalia," courtesy of Phil Crain. Many concluded that this was a government operation, considering the FBI magically uncovered the IxResearch hidden offshore accounts as well as the money from Nick's Metrix Technologies scam. Most investors got their money back, and the government agencies quickly appropriated the title of the heroes.

A year later, and Nick is still labeled "the evil master-mind" behind the biggest crypto scandal. Phil Crain became a semi-celebrity. I'm sure his acting career will skyrocket now that he's out of prison.

I put the magazine aside, feeling somewhat triumphant about the cover-up but slightly upset about the fact that I will never get all the answers about Julien.

As I wait for my pastries to be wrapped, I lean on the counter and stare out the window. At the café across the street, a man at a table catches my attention, his familiar face whipping me back in time. Goose bumps cover my skin at the sight of him, though it's hot in the bakery.

It can't be...

He's dressed in the true Santorini fashion—linen pants, white loose button-up over a muscle tank, sunglasses. I would've thought he was a hallucination if I didn't know his mannerism so well, his toned body, confident stance as he gets up, the sharp jaw, the way every movement seems calculated and on point when he tosses money onto the table and starts walking away.

"You gotta be kidding me," I murmur, not believing my eyes. "Christina, I'll be right back!" I say to the bakery owner and dart outside.

Maybe this is a mirage. I've thought about Julien so much in the last year that my mind might be doing tricks. But I have to make sure. So when I see him turning the corner into a narrow side street, I dart after him.

I find the street empty. I keep walking, peering into the distance, but after a minute or so, I give up, discouraged. Maybe I've completely lost my mind.

"Hello, Natalie."

The soft voice whips me around, and the man in white

steps out from behind an archway. He takes off his sunglasses, a smile playing on his tanned face as he takes slow steps toward me.

"Long time no see," he says in a voice that makes my head spin.

My knees go weak. I try to say something, but the words get stuck. My heart beats so loud that it makes the rest of the world fall away.

"It *is* you," I finally manage to say, and despite trying to hold it back, my lips spread into a grin.

JULIEN

She looks lovely. Sun-kissed skin. Long, loose hair swept over her right shoulder. Jean shorts and a loose white tank, covering a lime-green string bikini top. The sight of her so close to me makes a smile pull at my lips.

I've watched her for a year. Mostly on public cameras. Occasionally, on the streets. I was making sure she was safe and had no tail, though, as per my intel, the FBI hadn't figured out who was the housekeeper mentioned by Phil Crain. All he knew was that her name was "Natalia." The composite sketch was general at best. So were the ones of the other personnel at The Splendors. Phil took on the Rosenberg role so close to heart that he indeed thought he was above everyone else, including the staff.

This is the closest Natalie and I have been to each other in a year. But this time, when she looks at me, her gray eyes glint with delight.

Am I imagining it?

I study her face for any trace of bitterness, but there's none. Her full lips slowly spread in a smile, though the tiny vein on her neck pulsates with the speed of hummingbird wings. She's nervous, though she shouldn't be.

"It *is* you," she says, not hiding her excitement. "I thought I was hallucinating…" A quiet laugh leaves her lips, then she goes quiet for a moment, her eyes roaming my face. "How have you been, Julien?"

I know everything there is to know about her by now. Following her to Greece was intentional. I have a lot to discuss with her, but I start with the basics.

"It's Luke," I say, carefully studying her reaction. "My name—it's Luke."

"Luke," she repeats, making something flare up inside me. It's too early to expect her to trust me, but, damn, the way she says my name is delicious. I want to hear her say it one more time.

"Nice to see you again," she says. "Luke," she repeats, as if tasting the sound of it.

"How are you, Natalie?"

She chuckles, the sound of it warm and friendly, though she knows this is just small talk, that this meeting is not a coincidence.

Natalie almost jeopardized our entire operation a year ago. Too nosy, too brazen, too quick-witted—she came in like a storm, an unexpected intruder into our meticulously put together crew. It was a chore to keep an eye on her at all times, making sure she didn't tip off Nick by accident, didn't get involved with him or Rosenberg, or get in trouble. Poor Rita—a.k.a. Rosalie—tried intimidation, then scare tactics, then a one-on-one talk, then begged us all in tears to fire Natalie before something happened to her too.

At the end of the day, Natalie ruled everything out in the best way possible.

It's a proven fact that some seemingly unnoticeable things often change history. In science, it's molecules. In modern warfare, it's information. In everyday life, it's the smallest people who can cast the biggest shadows, causing the biggest impact.

A year ago, this courageous woman walked into The Splendors, and everything went haywire—my plan, my calculations, and somewhere, within a span of five days, my vow to never let pretty, smart women get in the way of my work.

But Natalie is a firecracker. She also deserves to know a lot more about what went down at The Splendors.

In time, I will tell her about Rita, whose husband had invested in Nick's enterprise years ago and had gone bankrupt, losing all their savings. When he found out he had cancer and no money for the treatment, he killed himself.

Will, a.k.a. Walter, is my sister Emily's fiancé and a cyber-security consultant.

Sagar, Dave, Steve, and the catering crew, all operating under aliases, were the team who had worked hard and for a long time to expose Nick, gain access to the stolen money, and return it to the investors. All of them had suffered at his hands in the past.

Soon, Natalie will learn that the night her friend Cara got in the car with Rosenberg, she called him "Phil," and Nick did what he did best—getting rid of witnesses. My sister, Emily, was monitoring the hidden cameras at The Splendors and listening in on the conversation through the bug in their car. She located Cara when they left her at the bus stop and made an anonymous 911 call. If she hadn't, Cara probably wouldn't have made it.

For a moment, I get lost, gazing at Natalie. Here, on Santorini, she is not an accomplice or liability but just a young woman, almost a stranger, pretty, charming, and someone I'd love to know better. I hope there's still a chance.

"Why do I have a feeling that running into you is no coincidence?" Natalie asks as she cutely squints at me.

"It's not."

I arrived on the island the same day as she and her friend. But I needed to get her alone so I could tell her the reason for this meeting.

"How is Greece treating you?" I ask, starting with a casual question.

"I think you know the answer. As well as who I'm here with and how long I've been here."

She's right, and I'm glad she's still in a good mood, no trace of anger in her eyes.

She tips her chin at me. "I'm sure you didn't come here because you wanted to see me. So?"

"And if I say I did?"

She purses her lips, trying to hide the smile that hasn't left her lips since she saw me. "Then I'd say I'm flattered. But you aren't telling me all of it."

"Fair enough," I say. "Remember the hard drive from the closet? The one you tipped us off about?"

She doesn't respond, but I know she remembers.

"That turned out to be Nick's crypto wallet," I explain.

"ErFi?" she prompts. Good, she knows what I'm talking about. "That stuff is still valuable after everything went down?"

Apparently, she has no idea. "Its value exploded in the last year."

Her expression changes with realization. "What are you telling me?"

"It's worth a lot of money."

"How much money?"

Her lips part as she waits for the answer, her intense gray eyes on me. I hope she doesn't have a heart attack when she finds out that she'll soon become a very wealthy woman.

"How much are we talking about?" she repeats impatiently.

I stall, savoring this moment, and she widens her eyes at me. "Stop teasing!"

"A lot," I answer.

That's an understatement. The value is a little over forty million, all Nick's personal stash. Karma is a patient vigilante. In our case, it turned out to be a generous fairy godmother. The money will be split among The Splendors' crew, including Natalie and Darla's family. But it's too early to tell her that. I need to know I can trust her. I hope I can. I want to. For the last year, I couldn't get this woman out of my mind.

Natalie sets her hand on her hip, and a smile finally breaks free on her lips.

"So, what, you flew to Europe and came to Santorini to tell me that you want to give me money?"

I shrug. "Something like that."

"You could've sent it in an envelope," she says, her eyes narrowing in suspicion, though her smile doesn't fade.

Clearly, she's underestimating what I mean by "a lot."

"It's a little more complicated than that," I say.

"I've gathered that you are a complicated guy, Julien."

"Luke," I correct her.

"Right, Luke. See?"

I'm smiling. She's smiling. It's really cute, and I can't tear my eyes off her.

"I have to warn you," I say. "Converting that crypto into cash has to be inconspicuous. It's a long-term project."

"And that's a problem?"

"Not for me, no."

I swear, her smile is flirty. Plus, standing in the middle of an empty Santorini street with her, early in the morning, feels like a romantic getaway.

"Well," she says, twirling a strand of her hair around her forefinger—like I said, flirty. "We have to talk it over, don't we? Would you like to have breakfast together?" She nods in the vague direction of the next street.

My heart skips a beat. "Breakfast?" I grin like a fool.

"Sure." She chuckles. "We are on vacation, right?"

"Breakfast sounds great," I say, unable to hide the smile plastered all over my face.

She turns and starts walking, and I follow. For the first time, I let her lead the way. "You know what sounds better?" she asks, smiling over her shoulder at me. "That you don't seem like you're about to ditch me for another year."

I laugh, following her.

This sounds like a possible date with this beautiful, resourceful spy. I'm in.

Read on for a sneak peek at

LOVE, MOM

PROLOGUE

I've never hurt a single person. But right now, I want to punch the face staring at me from the national newspaper's front page. A picture of *her*, with that signature red lipstick and long raven hair. The pretty face of a monster.

BESTSELLING AUTHOR FOUND DEAD

Elizabeth Casper, 43, better known around the world as E. V. Renge, the author of gritty thrillers, was found dead in what appears to be a "freak accident."

She is survived by her beloved husband, Ben Casper, and their twenty-one-year-old daughter, Mackenzie Casper.

The world is in shock at the tragic loss of the talented soul gone too early. Fans all around the world gather for a massive tribute to the literary genius.

Oh, the lies...

The cold smile taunts me from the newspaper in my trembling hands, and I have the urge to carve it out and wipe it from my memory.

She had it coming.

She deserved to die.

I just wish it had happened sooner.

ABOUT THE AUTHOR

Iliana Xander is the author of the psychological thriller *Love, Mom*. She's been writing stories since she was a teen and has published over twenty novels in various genres under different pen names. Secrets, heartbreaks, love, envy, and twisty twists—you'll find it all in her books. When she's not writing, she is traveling the world or making crazy art.